Summer Road Trip

Rocky Road

BY MELANIE DOWEIKO

EPIC Escape

An Imprint of EPIC Press
abdopublishing.com

Rocky Road
Summer Road Trip

Written by Melanie Doweiko

Published by EPIC Press™
PO Box 398166
Minneapolis, MN 55439

Cover design by Christina Doffing
Images for cover art obtained from iStock
Edited by Rue Moran

LIBRARY OF CONGRESS CATALOGING-IN-PUBLICATION DATA
Names: Doweiko, Melanie, author.
Title: Rocky road/ by Melanie Doweiko
Description: Minneapolis, MN : EPIC Press, 2018 | Series: Summer road trip
Summary: High school bandmates Shawna, Rev, and Cass are offered their very first gig.
   The only problem is, it's two states away and they can't get their parents on board. So
   they do what any rock-'n'-roll band would: sneak out! As they race against time—and the
   punishment that's sure to come after them—they find that life on the road is much stranger
   than they'd imagined.
Identifiers: LCCN 2016962616 | ISBN 9781680767247 (lib. bdg.)
   | ISBN 9781680767803 (ebook)
Subjects: LCSH: Adventure stories—Fiction. | Travel—Fiction.
   | Garage rock music—Fiction. | Parent and teenager—Fiction | Young adult fiction.
Classification: DDC [FIC]—dc23
LC record available at http://lccn.loc.gov/2016962616

For my mom, who would totally have done this if she had been in a band as a teenager

Chapter One

THE GUITAR SINGS AND SHAWNA SINGS ALONG WITH it. She feels her heart beating to the rhythm Cass is banging out. There are lights, there are people, there's a microphone in her hand that didn't come from a thrift store. She's on a stage—a real stage!—singing Rev's lyrics about running away.

Well, it's *sort* of a real stage. It was erected last night: a bunch of crates with a fancy top. And only some of the people are listening. Most of them are milling about the other attractions of the fair. And the lights were only turned on because it was starting to get dark.

Shawna can't say that she's disappointed. It's an improvement over her garage. They have actual exposure here. Anyone might be listening! Who knows who had shown up at the fair today, expecting to just be contributing to the fight against breast cancer (Never Forget Nina Clarke), only to be blown away by the magnificence of the Beauty School Dropouts?

As Shawna sings, her mind wanders to what recognition might get her and her band. Fame! Money! Fans! Everything a teenager could ever want. She knows what Rev is going to say: "It's not realistic, Shawna. Stop daydreaming up impossible scenarios. You're only setting yourself up for disappointment."

Well, phooey to that! Rev said that when Shawna suggested the idea for a band, too, and look at them now! Rev didn't even know how to play guitar back then. Without Shawna's help, Rev wouldn't be up here right now, and her songs would still just be poems and tunes she hummed softly to herself, so Shawna will set herself up for as much disappointment as she pleases. It keeps her working, keeps her wanting to achieve a goal. Imagining that things are impossible only makes her feel like she's already been defeated.

She finishes the song to a smattering of applause and the band leaves the stage. They're set to do a few more songs, later, but they've earned a dinner break. Free food! That was the best they were going to get for a charity gig, but Shawna doesn't mind. Neither does Cass. Free food always tastes better in their books. Rev usually says that it's all in their heads. Cass usually takes that time to make some kind of rude hand gesture at her.

"I think they like us!" Shawna says, patting her dark, kinky hair to make sure everything is still where it's supposed to be and taking a long drink of water.

"Hardly anyone was really listening," Rev says, tossing a can of soda between her hands.

"Who cares?" Cass says, taking a bite out of a pow-dered-sugar-coated funnel cake. "At least we got out of that stupid garage."

"Hey! Respect the garage," Shawna says, pointing at Cass with her water bottle. "A lot of really famous bands started in garages! We're a part of a long, noble tradition."

"And a lot of bands never got *out* of those garages," Rev points out.

"There, like I said!" Cass says, mouth full. "Glad we got out of that stupid garage. It smells like dog crap and that step is hard to wheel over."

Shawna rolls her eyes. It seems as if the duty of "dreamer" has, once again, fallen to her. "Ugh, you guys aren't *getting it*," she says, "and we put a plank over that thing for you."

Cass gives her a flat look. They all know it's not sufficient, but it's the best that they have. At least the stage, today, is wheelchair accessible.

Mrs. Johnson walks up to them. After hearing about them from her son, Timothy, she negotiated with their parents to let the BSDs play at the fair.

"Yeah, they're in a band or whatever," Timothy probably said, not looking up from his text conversation with his latest girlfriend. Even the teachers couldn't get that boy off his phone.

"Hey, girls!" Mrs. Johnson says. Cass rolls her eyes. "How's everything going? Good? Need anything?"

"We're good, Mrs. Johnson," Shawna says, matching the woman's smile, knowing that she cares, that she's trying. She got the BSDs a stage, at least. Shawna can't fault her for much after that.

"I could go for one of those hot dogs, over there," Cass says, intentionally choosing the farthest vendor from where they are sitting.

"You got it, sweetie!" Mrs. Johnson says, a flash of pity in her eyes. Shawna knows how much Cass likes to push the limits of people's pity, so she pinches Cass's arm before she can open her mouth to do so.

"You girls keep up all the good work!" Mrs. Johnson says as she walks away, giving the band a double thumbs-up. "We appreciate you!"

When Mrs. Johnson turns away, Cass punches Shawna in the arm.

"Ow!" Shawna says, rubbing it. For as small and scrawny as Cass is, she hits hard.

"The heck was that for?" Cass asks.

"Oh, come on, she knows how you get," Rev says.

"I have every right!" Cass says, folding her arms.

"We know, Cass, but that woman did us a favor," Shawna says. "We can't just be rude to her."

"If bein' in a band means kissin' up, I don't wanna be a part of it," Cass grumbles.

"Door's open," Rev mumbles into her soda can. She was against inviting Cass into the band in the beginning, insisting to Shawna that it was "their thing." But Cass is an amazing drummer and Shawna trusts her instincts. Besides, both Rev and Cass needed more friends. What better way to hit two birds with one stone?

"What did you just say, you . . . ?!" Cass says, only to be interrupted by Shawna coming between them, slinging an arm across both of their shoulders, an awkward arrangement considering how tall Rev is and how much shorter the chair makes Cass.

"Hey! Kiddos," Shawna says, "let's look at the positives here: We got our first gig! And we got paid!"

She glances at the funnel cake still sitting in Cass's lap. "Technically."

Rev and Cass follow her gaze to the funnel cake. With a small smile, Cass shrugs and stuffs her face with another piece of it.

"Better than nothing," Cass mumbles through a mouthful of fried dough, a puff of powdered sugar coming out with the words.

"Yeah," Rev mutters, looking away and tucking her short, brown hair behind her ear, "better than nothing."

In the near distance, a girl comes tripping towards them at full speed. Shawna squints. "Is that Junie?" she asks.

"Didn't she say she wasn't coming?" Rev asks.

"Well, yeah, but she said it in that way that meant she *was* coming, you know?" Shawna says.

Rev's brow furrows. "No . . ."

"That girl needs some dance lessons or gymnastics training or something," Cass says, watching her with amusement. "*I'm* more graceful on my feet than she is."

"*You guys!*" Junie is shouting. "*Oh my Go—osh you guys!*"

As much as Junie isn't able to catch herself physically, she still manages to keep herself from taking the Lord's name in vain in front of a large group of Good, Church-Going Christian Parents. Shawna is impressed.

Still, Junie nearly face-plants as she gets to them. Shawna manages to catch her before that happens.

"Hey, Junie," Shawna says, helping her back to her feet. "You seem excited."

"Well, duh, I'm excited!" Junie says. She's a burst of energy in too small of a container, or perhaps one that's too lanky. Her attempts to assist Shawna in her efforts to get her back to her feet only make Shawna's job harder as she flails or overreaches. It's like trying to hold onto a puppy that's seen a ball fly past or a toddler who wants to escape. A very tall puppy or toddler.

When Junie's finally stabilized, she begins to bounce. "Oooh, you guys! My aunt is here!" she says.

"Which one?" all three band members say in

unison. Junie's father has seven sisters and Junie speaks of each and every one of them intimately.

"Elle!" Junie says. "My auntie Elle! She owns a club called the Angry Whirlpool a couple states away and oooh, my gosh you guys!" She giggles and bounces some more.

"Out with it, already, girl!" Cass says. "You're killing us with this suspense."

"She likes you guys!" Junie says. "She really, really likes you! She likes you so much, she wants you to play at her club!"

Silence reigns among the girls as they process what they've just been told.

"Dang," Cass says.

Shawna couldn't have put it better herself. The first time they manage to get out of the garage and play for a crowd, they get offered a gig on a slightly more real stage with people who would actually be listening rather than milling about. She covers her mouth to keep herself from screaming, a face-splitting smile growing beneath her hands.

"You guys, it's going places! You could actually be going places! I told you! I always said you were awesome! I told you!" Junie's bounce speed has increased tenfold, the only outlet for her excited energy.

"You've always called us losers, though," Rev says, her expression difficult to read. She must still be processing things. It's quite a shock and it's happening so fast that even Shawna's head is reeling with giddiness. If things keep going like this, the Beauty School Dropouts will be famous within the next year!

Junie springs over to hug Rev. "Because you are! In the best way! You're the most winning losers on the planet!"

The statement makes no sense, but the sentiment does. Shawna allows herself a little squeal and joins the hug. Cass laughs and pats her back. For all Cass's talk of quitting, she sure seems excited.

Rev's memo to be excited must have been lost in the mail, though. "You said that club your aunt owns is a couple of states away, right?" she asks.

"Yeah, so?" Junie asks.

"How are we even going to get there?"

"I got a van," Cass says, "one o' them big, ol' wheel-chair vans. And since this baby folds up," she pats the chair she's sitting in, "we'll have plenty of room for all our instruments and junk!"

Shawna turns and high-fives Cass.

"Okay, but what about our parents?" Rev says, breaking away from Junie's hug.

"What *about* our parents?" Cass says, rolling her eyes.

"They're never gonna let us do this," Rev says.

"You're really killing the mood, here, Rev," Cass says, her excited smile moving towards an annoyed frown.

"Yeah, I'm sure it'll be fine!" Shawna says, not sure. Their parents allowed them to form this band, were supportive enough, but they always looked on it as a kind of phase. All three of the band members knew this. It was something about their tone of voice when they talked about the band, something about the way they kept suggesting other activities.

But Shawna doesn't want to think about that right now. She wants to bask in the joy of the opportunity, she wants to dream.

"No, these are things that we need to think about!" Rev says, pacing now. "We can't get ourselves all worked up over something that we might not even be allowed to do. Where is this club of your aunt's anyway?"

"Indiana," Junie says, a little sheepishly.

"*Indiana*. That's . . . " Rev pauses, doing calculations in her head, "a two-day drive! At *least*. Do you really think that our parents are going to let us do that? At all? I've never even been out of this state."

"Just because *you're* boring . . . " Cass mutters.

"Okay, okay, let's all just calm down," Shawna says. She hates to admit it, hates to kill the vibe, but Rev is right. This is a pretty big deal. It's something they need to think about. Rev is pacing. Cass is leaning her cheek on her fist. Junie is fidgeting.

"We'll all talk to our parents about this when we get home tonight," Shawna says, then holds up a hand when she sees Cass's smirk. "But! We're going to have to agree on what we're going to tell them." Cass's expression turns bored again.

Cass might be the tipping point of this operation, always picking fights with her parents. On some level, Shawna can understand, but this is not the time. This is a time for careful planning and delicate nudging. Shawna looks around at her bandmates: Rev is a nervous wreck, Cass is vindictive, and Shawna, herself, is overenthusiastic and insistent.

They're screwed, but Shawna refuses to give up. This could be their shot! She pulls her bandmates and Junie together, and they plot.

Chapter Two

"No," Shawna's Dad says.

She expected this. She had planned for this. "But don't you love and support me? No matter what I choose to do?" Shawna says, calling upon her best puppy dog eyes and aiming them in the direction of her Papa. A softer man than his husband, he had been the one to help her clean out the garage when she said that she was starting a band.

"Of *course* we do," her Papa says, putting a hand over hers. "But . . . your father's right."

Her Dad nods, gruff expression saying *Yes, of course*

I am. "No means no," he says and turns back to scraping cheese off of a dish.

"But, Papa, *please!*" Shawna continues to focus on her more lenient parent, hoping that she can break him. That's what she was counting on back when she made this plan with her bandmates. There are crocodile tears in her eyes. Well, they're crocodile tears for the most part. She might actually cry if she's not allowed to go, and Shawna makes a point to never cry. She can see her Papa's lip trembling. She's got him right where she wants him, she just needs to go in for the kill. She squeezes his hand and looks him in the eye.

"It's really important to me," she says. Her Papa lets out a small, indecisive noise and looks to her Dad. They all know that her Papa can't stand up to this kind of onslaught.

Her Dad sighs and walks over to the table. "Shawna," he says, "we love you, and it's because we love you that we don't want you doing this."

"But—!"

Her Dad holds up a hand to stop her from going on. "You're sixteen. You need to be focusing on school."

"School's not even in—!"

"Shawna," he interrupts, sterner this time, "let me finish. You're not old enough to run off to some club three states away. You're not even old enough to be in a club! Much less play in one. What if something happens?"

"You could come with." Shawna didn't want to suggest this. It's a last-ditch effort. If her parents go, everyone's parents will want to go. Rev's mom is untrustworthy and Cass's parents are overprotective.

Oh, they're so screwed.

"We would love to!" her Papa says. "But we have work."

"And we can't just cancel on such short notice," her Dad continues. "Speaking of, what kind of gig gives you such a short time frame? Sounds suspicious to me."

"It's Junie's aunt," Shawna says. "I trust Junie! You guys trust Junie. She's great."

"She *is* a great kid," her Papa says.

"Yes, but what do we know about her aunt? I've never met her. Your Papa's never met her. *You* probably only met her last night!"

He's got her there. She didn't *even* meet the woman last night, but Junie talks about her family so much she feels like she already knows them.

"The answer is *no*, Shawna," her Dad says. "That's final. Get it through your head."

Shawna shoves her chair away from the table and storms up to her room. She hears her Papa's shout of "We love you, honey!" follow her before she slams the door and collapses onto her bed. She screams into her pillow and takes a few moments to keep herself from crying.

This is the Beauty School Dropouts' opportunity! Their chance to reach a larger audience! To get their voices heard and to do what they love and have been dreaming of! Why can't her dads see that? What is so important about school if her band is able to make it big? Why are they so worried? She's sixteen! She can handle herself. She keeps Rev and Cass from tearing each other's throats out on a daily basis! She'd be able to handle a little trip across state lines.

She wonders if the others are faring any better. They promised that they would contact each other once they had spoken to their parents. Shawna takes out her phone and texts their group chat.

my parents said no. can u believe that!

A second later, a message from Rev appears.

Mine too. Im sorry Shawna. :(

wat r we gonna do? Shawna texts back.

UGH I H8 MY PARETNS! Cass texts.

urs say no too? Shawna asks.

YA THR LAME AND STUPID Cass texts.

Shawna figures Cass got into another fight with her parents, even though she promised not to. She screams into her pillow again. Screwed. Totally screwed.

She can't let this opportunity pass them up. She can't! There has to be some way to make their parents understand, some way to get them to agree . . .

Or maybe . . . maybe they don't need their parents

to agree after all. Maybe they could—and Shawna feels guilty just thinking about this—sneak out?

She texts her bandmates before she can lose her nerve.

i have an idea

tell Cass texts.

u have the keys to the van rite? Shawna replies.

ya Cass writes.

so lets just take it Shawna texts.

Her phone lights up with a series of NOs from Rev, covering Cass's enthusiastic YES!!!

Rev is nervous. Shawna is nervous, too, but Cass was right. They need to get out of that garage. She pulls up Rev's contact information and calls her.

"This is a bad plan," Rev says as soon as she picks up.

"Look, I know it's risky," Shawna says, "but we might not get another opportunity like this. Not for a long time, at least."

"Can't we just wait? Our parents will kill us!"

"If we wait now, all we're ever gonna be doing is

waiting. I don't really like going behind our parents' backs, either, but they gave us no choice. Come on, girl. People deserve to hear your music. It's time to Rev it up."

Shawna got Rev to do a lot using that phrase, ever since they were kids. So much so that it became her nickname. She dragged Rev onto roller coasters, convinced Rev to learn guitar so she could play the music she was always humming to herself, and got her to help create the BSDs.

She can practically hear Rev turning things over in her mind on the other end of the line.

"Are you sure it's time for that?" Rev asks.

"Why not? I've seen you. You love the music. You love playing it. This is that, just at the next level."

Rev takes a breath. "Okay," she says, "let's Rev it up."

"Yeah!" Shawna falls back onto her bed, pumping her fists in the air.

Chapter Three

SHAWNA CAN FEEL HERSELF SHAKING WITH THE beginnings of a cold sweat. In theory, jumping out of her bedroom window at night and onto the roof of her garage is a great idea. Looking at it now, her mind runs through a million possibilities of how it could go horribly wrong. What if she misjudges the distance? What if she loses her footing? What if the duffel bag slung over her shoulder tips her the wrong way?

She bites down on these fears and steps onto the windowsill. She looks down once again. What if the shaking is what does her in? What if some kind of survival response makes things worse instead? She closes her eyes and takes a deep breath.

In.

And out.

She turns onto her stomach and skooches backwards until only her upper body is still on the windowsill. She takes another deep breath.

In.

And out.

She pushes backwards and she's hanging out the window. Her feet don't reach the roof of the garage. She thought they would. She was betting on that. She panics for a second and considers screaming for her dads.

No.

She's come this far. She has to go all the way. She takes another, shakier breath.

In.

And out.

And she lets go of the windowsill.

Her feet touch the roof of the garage immediately.

She almost bursts into laughter. She's fine. She didn't fall, she didn't break a leg, and she didn't make too much noise.

She lowers her shaking body into a sitting position, waiting to see headlights in the dark. From here, she can jump onto the roof of Cass's van. She hopes. She looks down. Again, it seems farther than she bargained for. She tells herself that there's no helping that, now. She has to do what she has to do and if she doesn't, her dads can get her down in the morning.

She really hopes it won't come to that.

She pulls her duffel bag into her lap and watches the road, checking her watch every couple of minutes.

An hour later and the van still isn't there. *What is the hold up?* She texts Cass and Rev, but gets no answer. She's in the middle of convincing herself that her bandmates would never abandon her when she sees headlights coming down the road.

Cass's van pulls into the driveway. She cuts the engine, sticks her head out the driver's side window, and waves, stuffing some kind of chip into her mouth.

Shawna squints. "Did you stop for *snacks*?" she whisper-yells down at her.

"We can't go on a road trip without snacks," Cass whisper-shouts back up at her.

"You couldn't have come to get me first? I've been up here for an hour!"

"The gas station is on the way here! And Rev didn't help me!"

Rev pokes her head out of the other window. "I told her we should have gotten you first!" she whisper-yells.

"Did *you* get a snack?"

"Well, I mean, we were already there . . . " Rev says.

Shawna buries her face in her hands and lets out a muffled scream.

"We got you something, too!" Cass says.

"It had better have chocolate in it!" Shawna says. She scoots closer to the edge of the garage roof. In the hour that she was waiting, the shaking subsided, but it's back again. It's a far way down to the roof of the van, but she tries to tell herself that it's closer than she's making it out to be.

Rev climbs out of the passenger's side and holds her arms up. Shawna tosses the bag down and Rev nearly topples over when she catches it.

Cass snorts. "Hey!" she whisper-shouts up to Shawna, an amused grin never leaving her face. "If you hurt yourself, I've got a spare wheelchair!"

"Screw you!" Shawna whisper-shouts down to her. She is nervous enough already. She doesn't need to think any more about getting hurt. She takes a deep breath.

In.

And out.

And she dangles off the edge of the roof. She just did this, she tells herself. The drop will be shorter than she's imagining it, but she doesn't want to let go. She looks down.

Her grip tightens on the edge of the roof. She's not going to let go. She can't. The drop she saw was way too far. She tries to pull herself back up, but she can't do that either. She's stuck and her arms are starting to hurt.

She is about to scream and maybe start crying when she feels someone grab her legs.

"It's okay," she hears Rev say. "It's okay, I've got you. You can let go, it's fine."

Shawna feels like she can breathe again.

In.

And out.

She lets go and both girls topple onto the roof of the van. She wraps her arms around Rev in a tight hug. Rev hugs her back.

"See? It's all fine," Rev says. Her voice sounds as shaky as Shawna's body feels. Whatever kind of friendship-adrenaline had caused Rev to climb onto the van must be wearing off.

"Hey! Are you two done?" Cass says, leaning as far as she can out of her window. "We have a time limit, you know."

Shawna gives Cass an annoyed look. Where was this attitude when she stopped to get snacks? Shawna lets go of Rev and helps her up, then they help each other off of the roof of the van and open the back doors.

They pull the ramp and Cass's spare wheelchair out and go to open the garage. Shawna crouches at one end and Rev crouches at the other. They count in unison.

"One, two, three!" They lift the door. All three bandmates wince at the sound it makes, then stare at Shawna's house in dead silence for a moment. No lights flick on and no one marches out of the door, demanding to know what is going on, so they let out a collective breath and enter the garage.

They survey their equipment. Cass's drum set? Check. Speakers and microphones? Check. Miscellaneous wires? Check. Music folders? Check.

In.

And out.

"Okay." Shawna unfolds Cass's wheelchair and starts piling things onto it.

"Easy . . . careful . . . that's fragile . . . " is Rev's nervous refrain as she constantly looks over her shoulder for signs that they are being watched. Shawna rolls her eyes. If her parents weren't woken up by the garage door being opened, they probably won't wake up any time soon. Her Dad sleeps like a rock. And he snores, blocking out any sound her Papa might hear.

It takes four trips to get everything into the van. As they roll the bass drum up the ramp, completing their packing, Shawna goes back to survey the now-empty garage. She sighs. It's strange, seeing it like this. They had to bring their instruments to the charity event, sure, but that had felt so impermanent. This time, it feels like they won't be able to go back.

Cass taps the side of the van. "Shawna. We gotta go, girl! Reminisce on your own time."

Shawna turns to her, takes one last look in the garage, pulls the frayed rope to bring the door back down, and runs to join her bandmates. She closes the van door behind her, feeling the nervous tension coming off all of them in waves.

Cass starts up the van again. She backs out of the driveway and tears up the asphalt into the night. Shawna watches as her house, her garage, grow farther and farther away with a sense of dread and excitement.

She feels nauseated, though that might just be Cass's driving.

As soon as they're about to turn onto the highway, Cass rolls down the window and shouts into the night. "HECK YEAH! COME AND TRY TO STOP US! WHOOOOOOOOOOO!"

Rev looks at her like she's crazy, then turns back to Shawna to see if she shares the sentiment. Shawna just smiles and shrugs. She rolls down her own window and howls into the night with Cass. Eventually, Rev joins them.

Sweet freedom.

Sweet opportunity.

Chapter Four

THE NERVOUS EXCITEMENT OF THE NIGHT WEARS off as the sun rises high into the sky. By seven o'clock, Shawna's phone has rung a total of fifteen times and she's lost track of the amount of texts she's received. All from her parents. Rev and Cass's phones have been hit just as hard.

"I . . . I can't do it anymore!" Rev says on the twenty-seventh ring of her phone.

"Just turn it off!" Cass says, reaching for the phone. Rev holds it out of her reach. It's still ringing.

"Give it to me!" Cass demands. The van swerves as

she grabs at Rev's arm. Rev and Shawna scream before Cass rights the vehicle.

"Stop being so stubborn," Cass growls, eyes glued to the road now.

"Rev, seriously," Shawna says once her heartbeat returns to its normal rhythm, "just turn it off already."

"No! What if something important happens? What if someone *dies* o-or I miss something or we have to call the *police* or . . . "

"Nothing like that is going to happen and you know it," Cass says, knuckles turning white.

"How would you know!?" Rev says.

Shawna takes this moment of distraction to take the phone from her and shut it down.

"Hey!" Rev says, turning in her seat and reaching for her phone.

Shawna shoves it under her butt. "It's for your own good," she says.

"It's for all our own good," Cass says.

Rev folds her arms and turns back around, glaring out the window. Everyone is silent and tense. They have two days to get to their gig and they probably have their parents and possibly even the police on their tail. They're runaways now.

And isn't that just rock 'n' roll?

--- --- ---

Shawna is driving, Cass is in the passenger's seat, and Rev is in the back, squished up against their equipment. They all learned how to drive Cass's van as soon as they were able to drive, with the gas and brake being hand gears instead of at their feet. It's like a stick shift, only not like that at all.

Shawna has the classic-rock station playing quietly since Cass is sleeping and Rev was instructed to take a nap. Rev can't relax enough to do so.

"It's going to be great," Shawna says, watching her through the rearview mirror.

"It's going to be hell when we get back," Rev mutters into the window.

"Don't think about that," Shawna says. "Live in

the moment! Think about the stage! Imagine all those people cheering for us as we play the songs *you* wrote. Won't that be wonderful?"

Rev turns to look at Shawna through the mirror. "And what if that doesn't happen? What if they just hate us?"

"We can't just make decisions based on what might happen, Rev."

Rev grunts and turns back to the window.

"It's going to be great," Shawna repeats, both for Rev and herself. "You'll see."

– – –

Shawna has been driving for three hours. In the back seat, Rev finally managed to get some sleep and Cass is still snoozing away. Both girls snore, which is irritating, but Shawna tries to concentrate on the road and the low-volume music she has the radio tuned to.

Except it's on a commercial. She wonders why she

ever bothers with radio. She has plenty of music on her phone and Pandora is just as good an option.

Except Cass neglected to tell her where the aux cord is, and if Shawna turns her phone back on now, she knows that she will drown in the probably million-and-one notifications from her parents and other worried adults. Besides, she's not supposed to look at her phone while she's driving, especially when she's driving Cass's van.

She can feel her head pounding. Her eyes want to close. She didn't get any sleep last night at all. Not even while she was in the back seat. She had been too excited, too nervous, or too busy packing and unpacking and repacking her stuff. She's going to have to wake one of her bandmates up, and soon.

Rev has just gotten to sleep and probably won't be any more awake at the wheel than Shawna, so she doesn't want to wake her up. Cass, on the other hand, is nearly impossible to wake up. She sleeps like more than a log, or even a rock. The only reason she ever makes it to school on time is because she has incredible control over her internal clock. Of course, this also means that she can decide when she wants to sleep through class, but that's beside the point.

The point is that Cass is not going to wake up until whatever time she has deemed appropriate, another bit of information she neglected to share with Shawna and Rev.

Shawna is considering pulling into a parking lot so she doesn't crash the van when Cass yawns and stretches.

"Hey," Cass mumbles, smacking her lips. "Noon already?"

"Yes!" Shawna says. "And about time for you to take over."

Cass lets out a long groan. "What about Rev? Isn't it her turn?" she says.

"How do you know we didn't switch off while you were asleep?"

"Because you didn't." Cass cracks her neck. "It's her turn. She has to pull her weight."

"She just got to sleep."

"And?"

"And I'm *not* comfortable being driven around by someone who's half asleep, *Cass*."

"Whoa. Touchy. Sounds like she's not the only one who's half asleep, here. Why didn't you nap while I was driving?"

Shawna doesn't answer. She doesn't believe that Cass didn't notice the tension. Nothing less than a chainsaw would be sufficient to cut it. "I'll pull over at the next exit and we can switch," she says, instead.

The two are silent for a few minutes, nothing but the sound of the engine, Rev's snores, and the radio station switching between commercials and static.

"Are you two sure you're okay to do this?" Cass asks.

"Huh?" Shawna says, not allowing the odd question to distract her from looking for exit signs.

"I mean, I don't want to go through all this and have it be a bust, you know," Cass says.

"What are you talking about? They're gonna love us!" Shawna says. She feels like she just had this conversation with Rev, and Cass doesn't usually remind her of Rev.

"No, that's not what I mean," Cass says. Shawna can practically hear the eye roll. "I mean, I don't want to be halfway there and then have you guys chicken out on me."

"What?" She risks a glance at Cass this time, just to see if she's serious. "Come on. Why would we ever do something like that?"

"Hmm, let's think. Maybe because Rev is basically Mrs. Chicken."

"She's not a chicken," Shawna says, a stern note in her tone. "She's just nervous, is all. We all are."

"I'm not."

"Which is why you've been so quiet."

"What, you want me to snore even *louder*?"

"You know what I mean. Cass, you can't just pretend that this whole thing isn't nerve-racking. We snuck out, we basically stole your parent's van—"

"Uhm, this is *my* van. Not theirs."

"You can't say that this isn't new territory for us! You have to admit—"

"You're gonna miss the exit."

Shawna almost does and she doesn't have enough time to slow down before she gets to it. The turn shifts everyone and everything in the van. The tires squeal and a cymbal crashes to the floor. Shawna and Cass wince when they hear it.

Rev opens her eyes. She's groggy and confused and mumbling frightened, half-asleep nonsense. Cass turns back to look at her. She starts vocalizing a soft, slow song she learned in choir. Shawna recognizes it, so she harmonizes.

Soon, Rev is back to sleep and Shawna is parking at a gas station. "We're not gonna chicken out, Cass," she says. "You know us better than that. We're committed to this."

"Yeah, whatever," Cass says, still watching Rev, making sure she's asleep. She turns back to Shawna. "Just shut up and get out of the driver's seat so I can climb into it."

Shawna opens the door.

"And get me some coffee while you're at it." Cass digs into the glove compartment and hands her a wad of crumpled-up bills. "Don't want someone half asleep driving the van."

Shawna takes the money and heads into the gas station's convenience store.

– – –

Shawna is woken up by loud voices. Rev and Cass are awake together, and alone, so she should have expected it. She rubs the sleep out of her eyes, not troubled and not processing any of the angry words being thrown back and forth. She notices that the radio is all static now. They must have passed out of the broadcast zone. She starts flipping through channels while Rev and Cass argue.

Spanish station.

Spanish station.

Commercial.

Country station.

NPR.

Classical music.

"How could you have forgotten your guitar?"

Commercial.

Wait, *what?*

Chapter Five

SHAWNA TURNS AND SEES REV'S PANICKED EXPRESsion as she shuffles through everything they brought.

"Tell me you didn't," Shawna says. This can't be happening. This is their opportunity! They had a plan!

Rev doesn't look up, still digging through bags, even the ones too small for a guitar. "They have to be here . . ."

"'They'? What *else* did you forget?" Cass asks.

Rev looks up. "I . . . um . . . nothing . . . just the guitar . . . " She pauses. "Maybe . . . maybe we can just go back?" She doesn't sound as if she's even managed to convince herself.

"Go back? *Go back*?" Cass says, glaring at the road ahead. "We've been on the road for eight hours! *Eight hours*, Rev! You know what that *means*?"

"E-eight hours back?" Rev says.

"Yeah, eight hours back! You think we have that kind of time? That cuts a whole *day* out of our driving time! We're only in Wisconsin! We'll never make it! Not to mention that our parents are probably on our tail or have someone waiting at home. We'll never get out of the house again! *Ever*!" She lets out a frustrated grunt, shakes the steering wheel, then beats the horn with her fist a few times. A car beside them honks in annoyed response.

Cass rolls down the window. "*Screw you, buddy*!" she shouts.

Shawna drags her back into the car. "Calm down!"

"I am perfectly calm!" Cass shouts back at her.

Shawna shoots her a warning look, then turns to look back at Rev. The poor girl is shaking and close to tears. Shawna reaches out and takes her hand. "It's going to be okay. We'll just . . . get a new one!" she says.

"'Get a new one,' she says," Cass says with a bitter laugh. "Do you even know how expensive guitars are?"

"We don't have a lot of options, here. Look," Shawna places her other hand on Cass's shoulder, "we can make it through this. It's a minor setback. Really. All we have to do is find a music store or a second-hand shop, right? It'll be fine."

Rev looks down. "M-maybe this is just a sign that we should turn back," she says.

Shawna squeezes her hand and is about to say something encouraging when Cass speaks up.

"No way in hell. We're finding a place to get you a guitar." She takes a second to look Shawna in the eye. "I'm not lettin' either of you chicken out on me." She presses down on the gas and starts scanning signs for workable exits.

Shawna continues to hold Rev's hand and turns her phone back on for the first time since they left.

The amount of messages and voicemails is staggering. Even as she swipes them away, more and more appear. She lets out a frustrated grunt, turns the ringtone and vibration off, and tries to focus all her attention on her browser app. She only needs it for a few minutes, and then the phone is banished to the glove compartment again.

Music stores near me.

--- --- ---

"You want *how* much for that now?" Shawna says, staring at the sales associate in disbelief.

"Two hundred and sixteen," he says.

"We don't . . . we don't have that kind of money!" she says.

"That's your problem, kid," he says.

"It's a bust, Shawna," Rev says, still staring at the guitar, hand hovering just above it. "Let's just go."

No. No there has to be *something*. There has to be some way to bring the price down.

"Isn't there a student discount?" Shawna says.

"No."

"Band discount?"

"No."

Shawna glances over at Cass, who is twirling a drumstick in her hand, and decides to make one more last-ditch effort.

"Disabled discount?"

Cass's back straightens and she turns to glare daggers at Shawna. Shawna mouths an apology in her direction.

"If you kids aren't going to buy anything, you have to leave," the sales associate says.

The band members end up sitting on the curb, trying to think of other solutions.

"Three stores. You'd think at least one of them would price match," Shawna says.

"You'd think you'd learn that there's no such thing as a 'disabled discount,'" Cass says with finger quotes and a dirty look.

"I'm trying, okay!" Shawna says, matching Cass's look with one of her own.

They both hear a pathetic noise from Rev. She's hugging her knees with her head buried in them. Shawna sighs and wraps her arms around her.

"There's still a few second-hand stores," she says. "Maybe we'll find something there."

"Yeah," Cass says, putting a hand on Rev's head, "like I said, I'm not lettin' you guys chicken out on me." Her tone is much less hostile than the first time she brought it up with Shawna. It's almost fond, in fact. Shawna wonders at that, but doesn't get much time to as Cass smacks Rev on the back.

"Come on. Up you get," Cass says. "We're still on a time limit, and I need someone to help me over this curb."

Chapter Six

THE SECOND-HAND STORE ISN'T A CHAIN LIKE THE
Salvation Army, but a small, family-owned place
called The Secret Lotus. At least, it seems small from
the outside. Inside, it's so packed with other people's
odds and ends and who-knows-whats that it feels
bigger. Almost impossibly bigger. Looking around,
Shawna feels like she could spend at least a week here.

Old, worn books are stacked against the walls in
piles taller than she is. A table piled high with games
that haven't been seen or played in the last two decades
turns out to be a pool table. Hanging coats and sweat-
ers and other fluffy clothing create hallways that lead to

more items. Knickknacks and tchotchkes cover scuffed wooden shelves that are probably also for sale.

"We should split up," Shawna says once she's over her initial awe.

"You got it, Fred," Cass says. She tries to roll forwards and bumps into one of the shelves, shaking some necklaces loose and into her path. She narrows her eyes at the offending objects.

"Oh, you poor thing! Do you need some help there?" an older woman with a sweet smile asks. It's hard to tell if she works here or if she's just a regular. Her clothing and jewelry sure look like they were assembled from bits of other people's outfits, an amalgamate of the less-than-fashionable.

"I need you to shut up," Cass says.

At the woman's offended look, Shawna jumps in.

"She can handle herself. Thank you, though," she says. From the look on the woman's face, Shawna has at least halted her from giving Cass a lecture, which would not turn out well for any of them.

As the woman shuffles to the door, proving that

she's only a customer, Cass manages to find a broom in an umbrella stand and starts to sweep stuff out of her way. "Take *that* you little—"

"Are you sure we shouldn't stick together?" Rev interrupts.

"It'll be fine," Shawna says. She and Cass wander farther into the shop, Cass sweeping things away as she goes. Rev hesitates before nervously heading in another direction.

– – –

The Secret Lotus has a second floor and Shawna only manages to stumble into it accidentally. She hasn't seen anyone since that one older lady and she's starting to wonder if anyone works here at all. She has, however, seen several wonderful, ridiculously patterned dresses, a sculpture she intends to set over her mantel when she has her own house, and a bulky, bedazzled bracelet she intends to buy whether they find a guitar for Rev or not.

As she continues to explore the second floor, she passes by a mannequin in a rainbow paisley suit. A particularly life-like mannequin. As cliché as it sounds, she swears she can feel its eyes following her.

"Not creepy at all," she mutters to herself, trying to ignore it.

"Good! That's what I was going for," the mannequin says. Shawna jumps and nearly topples what might be a vase or maybe a distorted porcelain head. She rights it before "you break it, you buy it" sets in, then turns back to the mannequin. It has changed position, leaning forward on a cane it didn't have before, and it's smiling at her.

"Not creepy. More, eccentric!" the mannequin says with a wave of its hand. Shawna suddenly realizes— and she berates herself for taking so long to—that it's not a mannequin at all, but a person. A woman, maybe thirty or forty, short-cropped hair slicked back and blending into her pale skin just enough that she still looks somewhat fake.

"Wha—why were you standing there like that?" Shawna asks.

"Were you not listening to a word I was saying, child?" the woman responds, tapping her on the head with her cane. It's not hard enough to hurt, but Shawna feels like her personal space has been violated. She rubs the top of her head, still confused.

Another realization strikes: she's alone in a room with a weirdo in a paisley suit who had just been staring at her in silence. Had she been following her around the store? She tries to cover the wave of discomfort she feels with a smile, wishing she could just astral project outside of her "suspicious" skin tone. They're in a hurry. She doesn't need some kind of weird racial profiling right now.

"Well, Ms. 'Eccentric,'" Shawna says, using air quotes and what she hopes is a casual tone, "I'm kinda busy right now, so I'm just gonna . . . " She points towards the stairs and starts heading towards them with a little added speed in her step.

The woman thrusts her cane into her path. "If it's

something you're looking for, I'm the person to ask," she says with a little bow.

"Do you . . . work here?" Shawna asks, eyes glancing between her and the stairs.

The woman grabs a hat from a shelf, places it on her own head, then tips it and bows. "Owner and proprietor of this fine establishment, Alexandra Patton, at your service," she says.

Shawna watches her with confused amusement. The eccentricities and straight up ridiculousness of this woman seem to match the surroundings, but she never thought that someone like this existed. Besides, if she actually approached Shawna with the intent to help her rather than help her out of the store, then maybe she'll be able to find what Rev needs that much more quickly.

"Actually—" she begins, but Alexandra cuts her off with a swish of her cane.

"Wait!" Alexandra says. "Don't tell me. I know *exactly* what you want." She weaves through the room without touching a single item or shelf, reaches into a cluster of hanging clothes, and pulls out a dress. Shawna's eyes widen and her hand subconsciously makes its way up to cover her mouth.

It looks like it was ripped out of the fifties by force. The top is faded pink, the skirt is black with white polka dots, and it's torn in several places. It's torn just right, in fact, to display the blood-red fabric underneath. The sleeves have been cut off, leaving a jagged edge, and a big puff of red tulle fabric explodes from the back of the skirt.

It's perfect, perfect, *perfect* and exactly the kind of aesthetic she's been wanting to showcase with the band. Shawna lets out a small squeal to show how much she needs it. The squeal dies when she realizes that money is a thing that she doesn't have very much of right now.

"Yeah," Alexandra says, glancing at the dress, "the woman who dropped this off didn't seem to value it very much. And look! It's practically torn to shreds. I'd say about three Washingtons would cover it."

Shawna has to take a moment to process this. Three

dollars? For *that*? She tries not to look as excited as she is, lest Alexandra decide to jack the price up on her.

Alexandra holds the dress out on a finger to Shawna. "There's changing rooms just over there." She gestures with her cane in the direction of a half-hidden doorway just beside a lamppost.

Shawna takes the dress, a huge smile on her face as she skips towards the room.

– – –

A floor below and several feet to the right, Rev is searching the overcrowded walls for anything that might be useful. In the realm of musical instruments, she's found a snare drum, a tarnished flute being held up by a stone angel, and several different flavors of maracas, but no guitars or even anything in the same family.

She's beginning to consider calling this a failure and reporting back to Shawna and Cass when she hears it: a song she's never heard before being strummed out on an acoustic guitar. It's *beautiful*. She follows her ears to a room half-concealed by ponchos, bumping into a bookshelf and a mannequin on the way. She apologizes to both and pulls back the rough cloth of a poncho to reveal the person playing the guitar.

It's a woman in a blue paisley suit. She has pale skin and short-cropped, slicked-back hair, and her eyes are closed as if she's feeling the music she's playing. Rev stands in the doorway for a moment, enchanted, before the woman looks up at her.

"Do you play?" the woman asks without pausing her own playing.

"O-oh, um, well, yeah. Sort of. I mean, not really on acoustic. Electric, usually," Rev says, looking anywhere but directly at her. She'd always liked acoustic guitars, though. Even better than electric, but Shawna had always said they wouldn't work on stage.

The woman pulls a padded wooden chair out from behind the folding chair that she occupies. She pats the seat as if asking Rev to come and sit next to her.

"Oh! N-no, no!" Rev says with a nervous smile. "I

couldn't. I'm . . . I'm actually looking for something right now, so . . . "

"Then you've come to the right person!" The woman stands, leaning the guitar against the chair, places one hand on her chest, tucks the other behind her back, and takes a bow. "Owner and proprietor of this fine establishment, Alexandra Patton, at your service."

"Oh," Rev says, leaning back a little from the display, "well. That's . . . lucky."

"You want to know what I think you're looking for?" Alexandra asks with a wink.

"Well, uh . . . I, uh . . . " Rev takes a small step back. There's something kind of weird about all of this, but she can't quite put her finger on it. Maybe the odd surroundings are warping her perspective of the odd behavior of the owner.

"I think you're looking for exactly what you found," Alexandra says.

Rev pauses her slow retreat simply because that made no sense. She's about to tell her what she's actually looking for when Alexandra takes a step to the side and, with a flourish, indicates the acoustic guitar.

"Huh? Oh. N-no, no. Like I said, I-I don't usually play . . . "

"But the way you stopped to listen, dear. Oh! That's what's important. It called for you and you came. See how it shines in your presence?"

Granted, Rev didn't take a good moment to look at it. She only listened. It was producing a truly beautiful sound, though whether that was due to the guitar or the musician was still unclear.

She takes a moment to look at it now. The wood has a reddish tinge to it, a shine, like Alexandra said. Someone had clearly loved and cared for this guitar because it is not new. Not only is it sitting in a second-hand shop, but Rev can see a slight difference in color where some of the strings were switched out for better ones. It has a small, swirling, red-and-black design of a bird painted onto the front of it. Its aesthetic matches its sound: beautiful. She wonders if, *perhaps*, acoustic and electric guitars aren't that different after all. Maybe Shawna is wrong.

Suddenly, Alexandra is behind her, hands on Rev's shoulders. When had she moved? How long had Rev been staring at the guitar?

"Go on," Alexandra says in a low voice, "go answer the call." She gives Rev a gentle nudge in the direction of the guitar, but Rev doesn't need much nudging. She sits down in the chair Alexandra had previously pulled up for her and picks up the guitar. Oh! It fits into her arms perfectly! Like she imagines a mother feels when first given her newborn child. She begins to strum something that had been playing softly in the background of her mind for a year or so. Her eyes close, a small, serene smile graces her lips, and she loses herself in the music.

– – –

Much closer to the front door, Cass is not having such a good time. The broom she picked up only does so much to widen the narrow hallways of junk she's forced to traverse, looking high and low for a stupid electric guitar. She mumbles most of the curses she knows under her breath. The rest she says above it. She feels like a grizzled, bitter sailor, fighting her way through the ocean swells, looking for the elusive, magical object promised on an ancient map.

She decides to stop feeling like this. Playing pretend has never made annoying situations easier to bear.

As she comes to an armoire leaned against something she can't quite see, the image of a coffin comes into her mind. How creepy would that be? A coffin in a second-hand shop. As she attempts to pass the armoire, the coffin connection she just made becomes horrifying for a second as the door bursts open. She jumps and brandishes her broom, her fight instinct winning out as flight is nearly impossible. What steps out and farther into her way, however, is not a zombie or a vampire or anything like that, but a woman in a gold and black paisley suit.

Cass takes a deep, annoyed breath, though whether

she is annoyed with the woman or herself is unclear. She decides that she is annoyed with the woman. It makes things easier.

"Who the hell are you? What the hell were you doin' in there?" Cass asks, glaring at the woman.

"Alexandra Patton," she says with a bow, "owner and proprietor of this fine establishment. How may I assist you?"

"I don't need 'assistance,'" Cass says, glare deepening. "What I need is a stupid electric guitar so I can get the hell out of your stupid 'establishment.'"

"Electric guitar? Hmmmm . . . " Alexandra thinks for a moment, hand on her chin and elbow resting in her other hand. Cass didn't think anyone outside of cartoons and TV shows thought in that position. "I'm afraid we don't have any, at the moment," she says. "However—"

She is cut off by Cass brandishing the broom again, pointing it so that it's nearly touching Alexandra's lips. "Say that again," Cass says, anger boiling in her tone.

"That again," Alexandra says.

Cass resists the urge to smack her with the broom. "Don't be coy with me, lady, you know what I meant!"

Alexandra doesn't seem fazed by the potential violence held in Cass's hand. "We may not have any electric guitars, at the moment, but I believe I can find you something—"

"Nope! Shut up," Cass says, cutting her off again. "That's all I needed to hear or know. Thank you." Her tone does not hold any true thankfulness and the smile she flashes at Alexandra is the furthest thing from genuine. It soon morphs back into a frown accompanied by a glare and she turns around to assess her path out. "Stupid . . . " she mutters as she begins to use the broom to push her chair backwards.

Alexandra cocks her head. "You're a very rude child," she says, as if Cass is just the latest curiosity that has been pedaled through her door.

"Does it look like I care?" Cass says, not turning back to look at her.

Alexandra watches Cass struggle for a moment longer before using her long legs to step around and through the debris in Cass's way and end up *in Cass's way* again. "Allow me," Alexandra says. She takes hold of the handles on Cass's wheelchair.

For a second, Cass feels as if she's lost all control. Her grip tightens on the broom and she doesn't hesitate to smack one of Alexandra's hands with the handle. Alexandra jumps back in an exaggerated way that would be comical if Cass was in a comedic mood. As it is, she is brandishing the broom again, her knuckles almost white, keeping it between Alexandra and her chair.

"*Don't* you *touch* me!" she growls. "You *aren't* allowed to *do* that!" Cass thought this road trip would help her get away from treatment like this.

Alexandra blinks, rubbing her hand, then dips into another bow. "My deepest apologies," she says. Cass nearly drops the broom. Normally, she would have to keep fighting after something like that, if not with fists then with words. No one had ever just accepted the situation before.

"It would appear as if I have been ignorant,"

Alexandra says. "Do carry on and shout if you need me." She flits away and disappears somewhere behind a rack of cloaks.

Cass lowers the broom, watching the space, unsure how to feel.

She decides that the woman is still annoying and continues to back out.

– – –

Shawna admires herself in the mirror. The dress is a perfect fit, which is probably the most shocking thing about it. She's had the experience time and again: she finds the most perfect article of clothing, tries it on, and it's too big here or there, or too small in other places. She has an odd body type, she supposes, or at least one of the millions that clothing designers refuse to acknowledge.

She strikes a pose and hears applause. Alexandra is behind her in the mirror, a grin on her face. "It's gorgeous! Perfect! Superb!" she says. "You bring out all the best qualities in one another."

Shawna blushes and looks down at the dress, brushing imaginary dust off. "Thank you," she says with a giggle.

As she looks back into the mirror, striking another pose, she hears a distant "*Shaaaawwwnnaaa!*" She turns towards the sound, brow furrowed. That sounded like Cass, an angry and annoyed Cass, no less. She hops, skips, and jumps over second-hand items to get to the staircase. Alexandra is not far behind.

Cass is at the bottom, glaring up. As she looks Shawna up and down, the glare deepens. "Have you been playing *dress up*? What the *heck*, Shawna?" she says.

Shawna looks down at the dress, embarrassed now that she remembers what she came in for and how much time she wasted with this. She feels Alexandra's hands on her shoulders, supporting her in a way.

"Your friend was simply—" Alexandra begins.

"Hey!" Cass cuts her off. "I already told you, I

didn't wanna hear it!" She gives Alexandra the same up-and-down treatment she'd just given Shawna. "How many of those ugly suits have you *got*?"

"Oh, I wouldn't call them *ugly*," Alexandra's voice says, but not from behind Shawna.

Cass jumps and brandishes the broom. Alexandra, gold and black paisley suit and all, is standing right next to her.

"Wh-hat the . . .? Huh?" Cass holds her broom at the ready and glances between the two Alexandras until her expression falls into one of annoyed realization. "Twins," she says, lowering the broom.

"Oh, so you run this shop with your sister, then?" Shawna asks with a smile, not as phased as Cass seems to be. Twins aren't exactly a phenomenon.

"Yes," both women say at the same time.

Shawna giggles and starts down the stairs. Cass cringes away.

"So, what's your name, then?" Shawna asks of the gold-suited twin.

"Alexandra Patton, at your service," she says with a bow.

Shawna pauses her descent and turns back to the rainbow-suited twin. "Wait, but I thought *your* name was—" she begins, but Cass cuts her off.

"Shawna, we need to leave. Like, *now*," she says.

Shawna continues her descent and, once next to Cass, informs her in a low voice that she's being weird.

"Oh, *I'm* the weird one in this situation?" Cass says in a not-so-low voice. Shawna flashes the Patton twins an apologetic smile on Cass's behalf. Cass continues to glare at them.

"Hey, guys!" Rev's cheerful voice chimes in from behind them. Everyone turns to see her stumbling towards them with an acoustic guitar in one hand. "Guys, look what I . . . Oh." She pauses, glancing between the two Alexandras. Shawna and Cass follow Rev's gaze as she turns back to see a third Alexandra wearing a blue paisley suit, following behind Rev at a leisurely pace.

"Um . . ."

"I thought you said you were twins?" Cass says, turning back to the other two.

"Oh, no, no, no," the rainbow-suited one says. "*You* said we were twins."

"*We* say that we're triplets!" the gold-suited one says.

"There's not a quadruplet gonna come poppin' out of a closet is there?" Cass says, pushing open a nearby closet with her broom. When it reveals nothing but shelving full of bird sculptures, she lets out a relieved breath, then swings the handle of the broom around to point at Shawna. "Pay for your crap and let's get the hell out of this creepy death trap!"

"Oh, I wouldn't say we're creepy!" the blue-suited triplet says.

"More . . . eccentric!" the rainbow-suited triplet says with a sly smile.

Shawna sees something snap in Cass. Whatever she had to deal with while she was down here on her own, shoving things out of the way with a broom, this comment is the last straw.

"*You're creepy*! Creepy is what you are!" Cass says, pointing at the Alexandras. Both Shawna and Rev give Cass a look, but Cass doesn't seem to care.

Shawna heads back upstairs for her clothes and wallet, feeling the need to leave lest Cass starts smacking someone with that broom.

"Who gives all their kids the same name, anyway, huh?" Cass says, still pointing at the women. "Y'all are either lying or you come from a really weird and creepy family!"

"Cass, shut up," Rev says, hand over her eyes in annoyance.

"Me shut up? You shut up, Ms. 'I Forgot My Guitar at Home'!"

Rev cringes.

"You didn't even find the right thing in here!" Cass says, pointing to the acoustic Rev is subtly trying to hide behind her back. "You're just—"

"That's enough, Cass, seriously," Shawna says, returning. Cass glares at her, but grumbles and stops shouting. Shawna pays the rainbow-suited Alexandra for her dress and the guitar and the broom, knowing that no one is going to be able to pry it out of Cass's death grip and that Cass isn't going to put it down willingly until the shop is long behind them. The total comes to only ten dollars. One Hamilton. What kind of business model do these ladies have that allows them to sell this stuff so cheap?

"I'm sorry about her," Shawna whispers.

Cass smacks her with the broom. "I said *move it*! Come on, ladies, hop to!" Cass says. She sweeps the girls out the door.

"Come again soon!" the gold-suited Alexandra says, her tone amused and smug.

"*Screw you*!" Cass shouts, and slams the door behind them.

Chapter Seven

"**A**M I SERIOUSLY THE ONLY ONE OF US WHO thought that was weird?" Cass asks. Shawna is driving, back in her normal clothes. The dress and the broom are lying next to one another in the back of the van and Rev is plucking out a stiff tune on the acoustic.

"It was a second-hand store. A family-owned one. They're full of weird stuff," Shawna says.

"Not like that!" Cass says. "That was some . . . some kinda Greek myth death-trap thing."

"You're just upset that we spent so much time in there," Shawna says.

"Oh, and whose fault is that?" she says sarcastically.

"*Hmmm*, I *wonder*." She turns back to glare at Rev. Rev matches the glare and plays a wrong note on purpose.

"Okay, okay," Shawna says, "let's just focus on what's important. We gotta get Rev a guitar that she can play on stage."

"Right, because we have the money and the time to do more shopping. We've already wasted three hours and we're *still in Wisconsin*!" Cass says, folding her arms and turning to glare out the window.

"We'll figure *something* out," Shawna says, beginning to feel unsure herself.

– – –

An hour of driving and uncomfortable silence passes between the bandmates. Shawna has never seen pea soup, herself, but she's heard rumors of its thickness and is willing to bet that the tension in the car is about as thick, penetrated only by occasional soft notes from

Rev's new acoustic. After a while, low, distant music joins it.

"Hey, Shawna, can you turn the radio off?" Rev asks. "I'm trying to think through a tune and it's distracting me."

"Hey, Shawna, can you turn the radio up? I'm trying to listen but Rev's annoying voice is distracting me," Cass says.

"Hey, Shawna, can you tell Cass to go shove a—" Rev starts.

As Shawna reaches out to turn the radio up to full volume in an effort to drown them both out, she notices something. "It's not the radio," she says before Rev can finish.

"What?" Rev asks.

"It's not even on," Shawna says.

The bandmates roll down the windows and, sure enough, the music gets louder. They stick their heads out and it gets louder still. Alternative rock, wafting towards them on the rush of the wind.

"Where's it coming from?" Rev asks.

Her question is answered as the van crests a hill and traffic stops. A multitude of people have gathered in a park a little way down the road. Cars surround it on all sides, blocking any hope for street parking. A cop in an orange vest is directing traffic at the intersection just before the park.

As they approach her, Shawna can't help her curiosity. "What's going on?" she asks.

"Big concert," the officer says. "Some kind of charity thing or something."

"What charity?" Shawna asks.

"I don't know, girl, I just direct the traffic. Move along, now," the officer says.

Shawna does so, a little annoyed at the woman's tone, but as the music gets louder, she finds that she can't stay that way. It's enchanting, in a rock-'n'-roll way. She wants to get closer, to be inspired, to see who's singing. It sounds like a woman.

Cass snaps right next to her face. "Hey, let's get a move on. We got places to be," she says.

"Maybe we can just go in for a few minutes?" Rev

pipes in from the back seat. She's resting her head on the windowsill and seems to be just as enchanted by the music as Shawna.

"Are you two kidding me?" Cass says.

"Come on," Shawna says. "You love loud music and crazy crowds. Might help us unwind a bit." God knows, they all need it. Shawna doesn't think she likes the taste of pea soup. Besides, the gig is tomorrow night. They have time to get there. Right?

"Do I have to tie you both to the mast?" Cass says, "'Cause that's a siren song if I ever heard one! Eating away our precious time and *your* common sense!"

"You're still stressed because of the thrift store," Rev mumbles.

"No, I'm not!" Cass says, turning back to glare at her. "I'm weirded out by and pissed about the thrift store!"

"It'll be five minutes," Shawna says.

"Five minutes never means five minutes, especially when you say it like that about something like this," Cass says. "You know what? If you two idiots want to waste whatever time we have left, then fine! Go ahead! I'll just leave without you!"

"No, you won't," Shawna says.

"Yes, I will," Cass says.

– – –

Cass grumbles to herself in the midst of the crowd, trying her best not to enjoy the music and the people. Shawna was right: loud music and loud crowds are her thing, and this concert is both. The people—a majority of whom seem to be women, actually—are having the time of their lives. They're dancing, screaming along to the music, and someone is even crowd surfing.

Cass wants to crowd surf. But no. She can't give in. She has to stay bitter and stubborn. Her body, traitor that it is, though, is nodding along to the beat.

"Come *on*, Cass!" Shawna says, dancing by with a huge smile. "Join in! You know you'll love it!"

Cass turns her nose up and refuses to answer.

"YOU ALL HAVIN' A GOOD TIME?" the singer,

an Asian woman with short, spiked-up black hair, shouts into the mic. The crowd cheers.

"Let's hear that roar again!" She points the mic at the crowd, which obliges her. Some even let out animal roars. Cass continues to sit with her arms folded, glaring at some space ahead of her. As much as she loves seeing kick-butt Asian girls like her on stage, she's too annoyed with the situation to celebrate it.

The singer squints into the crowd. Cass looks up at her for a second, and she can swear that the singer is squinting right at her.

"Hey, you there," she says into the mic, "in the chair. You doin' alright?" She sounds concerned, genuinely so, and the crowd turns to try and find who she's talking to.

Cass clenches her teeth. "No!" she shouts, wondering if she's pitying her because of the wheelchair and hating her for it. She wants to leave, to get to the gig, to have a crowd of her own to shout to, to be cheered for because she got a crowd's hearts going with a drumbeat instead of being pitied by one. She can feel the looks this crowd is giving her. Pity is palpable, and she hates it. She hates this crowd, but she keeps her glare on the singer. This woman, the one who owns them. She can direct their attention in any way she chooses, and she decided to direct it at Cass.

Cass is not going to make it easy for her.

"Hey, why don't you come on up here, then, kiddo? Tell us something about yourself," the singer says.

The crowd cheers and clears a path, but no matter how hard they try to hide it, the pity is still obvious. This is not the first time, and it won't be the last, so Cass moves to wheel forward.

Shawna puts a hand on her shoulder and gives her a thumbs-up. She knows what's about to happen. It's happened before. Even Rev is giving her an approving look.

The singer may control the crowd, but she doesn't control Cass. When this is all over, that stage isn't going to belong to her anymore.

She wheels up to the stage and bumps against it on

purpose. "Wow," she says, deadpan, "no ramps. How surprising."

The surprise and confusion that flashes across the singer's face puts a small smirk on Cass's. *That's right, lady,* she thinks, *I ain't your average inspiration porn.*

The singer regains her crowd-pleasing smile (one with a hint of pity in it; *God* how Cass hates the pity) and hops down from the stage.

"Stooping to my level?" Cass says, sarcasm still strong in her voice. "Aw, you shouldn't have."

Another flash of confusion crosses the singer's face, but she continues on. "What's your name and pronouns, kid?" she asks and sticks the mic in Cass's face. Cass takes it right out of her hands.

"Cass," she says. "She, her, hers. What about you, adult?" She sticks the mic in the singer's face, thriving off of her confusion, but there's something else in her expression. Is she . . . impressed?

"Suki Gradstein," she says. "She, her, hers." She smiles. The crowd cheers. She's still in control.

"Tell me, Suki Gradstein, why did you call me up here?" Cass asks. She sticks the mic in her face again.

"You didn't seem like you were havin' a good time," Suki says.

"Yeah, well, that's because my friends are idiots." Cass can hear distant boos from Shawna and Rev, but ignores them. "But why did you *really* call me up here?"

"I wanted to see what I could do to help . . . " She sounds unsure, like she's starting to realize that Cass has something up her sleeve and is nervous for the reveal.

"So, what?" Cass says. "I get up here, spill my *tragic* life story, we sing a song or you make a donation or something, and the crowd gets to say, 'Gee willikers! That Suki Gradstein sure was great with that poor disabled kid! She's such a good, kindhearted person isn't she?'" Cass pauses to listen to the uncomfortable murmuring of the crowd. "Do you see where I'm goin' with this?" She sticks the mic in Suki's face again.

Suki is looking down at her like she's sizing her up.

"Yeah," she says, "yeah, I think I do, actually." She takes the mic from Cass's hand and Cass doesn't fight her. She could hear it in her voice: a kind of self-reflection, a coming to terms with things. Something Cass said had gotten to her, and that was enough for Cass to consider the stage taken.

Suki tosses the mic up to one of her bandmates and they start to play again as if some kind of unspoken instruction has passed between them. "Think you and your idiot friends can come talk to me for a second?" she says over the music.

That sounds, to Cass, like a chance to educate someone. More importantly, it sounds like a way to take her bandmates away from the concert, out of the fun zone and back on track. She nods and signals to the girls to come over.

– – –

Suki leads them to a van that has been spray-painted with the words YELLOW FEVER BREAK and a picture of an anime nurse girl hoisting up some guy's decapitated head. Suki opens the back and takes out a bottle of water, gulping down at least half of it before offering any to the bandmates.

Annoying them did not go the way Cass planned, as both Rev and Shawna are ecstatic to be talking to a woman who has command of a crowd that big and enthusiastic.

"What did you bring us here for, anyway?" Cass asks.

"I wanted to apologize to you somewhere I didn't have to shout over the music," Suki says. "You called me out for pitying you. I shouldn't have done that. You got some guts."

"I shouldn't have to prove that I have guts for you not to pity me," Cass says.

"Touché," Suki says, nodding. "I'm sorry." She leans forward a little. "The thing is, I've done stuff like this before, and no one's ever complained until now."

"Yeah, well, not everyone's got guts and not everyone's got a problem with it. We're not a monolith, you know," Cass says. "But every time you do it, you're telling disabled people that they're only worth the recognition their disability can get them, and you're telling everyone else that it's okay to pity them and use them as props to make themselves feel better."

Suki is nodding. She seems to be taking everything that Cass says to heart.

"I appreciate this," she says, "I really do. I'm a feminist, you know. At least, I try to be, and feminism ain't nothing without intersectionality. There's still a lot of stuff I don't know."

Cass nods, hating her less and less. "Yeah," she says.

Cass glances back at her bandmates. She's about to say something sappy and vulnerable, and she's hoping that the girls are distracted by something. Alas, they both have their full attention on Suki and Cass.

Cass sighs and braces herself. "Thanks," she says, refusing to make eye contact with Suki, "for listening. Not a lot of people listen."

She catches Shawna's soft smile and Rev's amused

one out of the corner of her eye and turns away from them with an annoyed expression.

"I know how you feel," Suki says, "but let's move away from the sappy stuff." She smirks and Cass almost lets out a chuckle. She clamps down on it before it can happen, though. She has an image to keep up.

"What brings you kids here?" Suki asks.

"Well, we're *supposed*," Cass throws a glare at her bandmates, "to be headed to a gig right now."

Suki breaks into an enthusiastic smile halfway through a sip of her water. "You guys are a band?" she says.

"Beauty School Dropouts," Shawna says, her smile bigger than Suki's and full of pride.

"Oh, my God! I love it!" Suki says. "Where are you headed?"

"Indiana," Rev says.

"Wow," Suki says, "that's a whole state away . . ."

"*Still*," Cass says. "We've been driving for almost a day, and we're already behind schedule."

"Well, what the heck are you still doin' here then?" Suki says.

"That's what *I've* been trying to say! But Dumb and Dumber here won't listen to me! Not to mention this one," she says as she pinches Rev's hand, "forgot her guitar at home!"

Rev rubs her hand, glaring at Cass, then smacks her shoulder.

Shawna gets between them. "It was an honest mistake," she says.

Cass is about to retort when Suki chimes in. "Well, if you need a guitar, I've got a spare."

The three bandmates turn to stare at her with wide eyes.

"Are you kidding?" Cass asks.

"It's right in the van, here," Suki says. "I can get it out now." She clambers into the back. After a few bumps and thumps, she returns with a guitar. An *electric* guitar, red with black flames licking at the sides and as shiny as if it were new. She hands it to Rev; Cass and Shawna's eyes remain fixed on it.

"I . . . " Rev begins, but is not sure where to go. She holds it as if someone has just handed her their child, no idea what to do and afraid she might break it. "I . . . we can't accept this."

"Um, yes we can," Cass says.

"Weren't you just talking about not wanting people to give you things out of pity?" Rev says.

"There's a difference between pity and generosity," Cass says. She has become very attuned to that difference over the years.

"Yeah," Suki says, "we all gotta look out for each other, right? If we don't, no one will."

Shawna bounces forward to shake Suki's hand. "Thank you!" she says. "Thank you, so much! You have no idea how much this means to us!"

"It's not a problem, really," Suki says. "This your first gig?"

All three of the bandmates nod.

"Yeah, I remember back when I was in your boat. Excited but nervous as hell." Suki chuckles. "You three go out there and you knock 'em dead! Me 'n' the Yellow Fever Breaks are rooting for you over here!" She holds up her hand and high fives all three of them, then shoos them away. "You got a gig to get to! Go on! Get!"

Chapter Eight

THE BANDMATES CONTINUE TO DRIVE FOR A FEW more hours, Rev getting a feel for her new guitar between sleeping in shifts.

As Shawna takes the wheel for her turn to drive, she finds that she can't fully focus on the road. "Um, guys? I'm starting to think that we may need some actual sleep," she says.

"What are you, a baby?" Cass asks, though the effect is ruined by a yawn in the middle of her sentence.

"If we keep trying to drive like this, one of us is going to fall asleep at the wheel or something and we're going to crash and die," Shawna says.

"I vote for not crashing and dying," Rev says, fully awake now, not that Shawna believes she'll stay that way long enough to drive.

"Fine," Cass says, trying to clamp down on another yawn. "We'll find some cheap roach motel and catch a few hours."

Within the next twenty minutes, they find one just off the side of the highway. It's a name they don't recognize, partially because most of the letters are unlit or busted. Shawna pulls into what she assumes is a parking space, gravel crunching under the tires, and hops out to crunch the gravel under her feet and talk to the front desk.

"Are you sure we shouldn't keep driving? Find another one?" Rev says, looking around. "This place seems really sketchy."

"Baby," Cass says.

"You already used that insult," Rev says without her usual enthusiasm. She hasn't stopped looking around.

"Screw you, I'm tired," Cass says, resting her head against the window.

"It'll be fine," Shawna says to both of them, cutting into whatever argument they're about to have.

Rev hugs herself and whimpers.

"Really. It'll only be for a few hours. Just some sleep, and then we're gone." If Shawna's being honest, she's a little nervous about this place herself. "Roach motel" was right. This place is a dump! The parking spots aren't marked and almost all the paint is peeling.

She walks up to the desk, where a girl about her age with bushy brown hair that comes down to her chin and light brown skin is leaning against the counter, reading a book and looking bored.

"Excuse me," Shawna says.

The girl looks up. Her eyes widen a bit. She places a bookmark in her book, closes it, and shoves it away without breaking eye contact with Shawna. "Need a room?" she asks with a smile.

"Yeah, just for the night."

"Aw. Not staying longer?"

"No, actually. We have to get back on the road in a couple of hours."

"We?"

"Yeah, me and my two friends."

"Well, we *might* have something." The girl lugs out a large, ancient-looking registry book and spends a few minutes scanning the pages.

Shawna glances back at the parking lot. The van is the only car there. She turns to look at the wall of keys hanging behind the door. Every single nail has a key on it. There is obviously no one else in this motel, so what's the delay?

"Your, uh, parents or employers make you look through that big book every time?" Shawna asks in an attempt to lighten her unease.

The girl looks back up at her, her finger halfway through scanning a line. "What are you talking about?" she asks.

"I mean, like, you know . . . no one else is here?" Shawna says.

"Well, obviously," the girl says. She goes back to scanning the book.

Shawna taps the desk with her fingers a few times. "So, then, your employers make you do it," she says.

"I don't have any employers," the girl says. She pauses. "Well, I suppose you could say that I'm self-employed, in which case, yes. My employers make me do it." She goes back to scanning.

There is no way she is self-employed. That would mean that she owns the building, and she can't own the building. She's Shawna's age.

Isn't she?

"How old are you?" Shawna asks.

"Fifteen," the girl says.

She's *younger* than Shawna's age! There is no way that this is legal. Maybe she's lying. Maybe Rev was right and this place *is* too sketchy to stay in.

"Room Ten," the girl says, breaking into Shawna's thought process. She turns the book around and hands a pen to her. Shawna hesitates, but takes it and signs the register. After all, what she and her bandmates are doing isn't exactly the most parentally supervised thing. Who is she to judge this girl?

She hands Shawna a room key. "Enjoy your stay!" she says. "If you need anything, my name is Cici and I'll be here all night." She wiggles her fingers at Shawna as she heads back to the van.

"You get us a room?" Cass asks when she returns.

"Yeah, it's . . . " She looks around at the doors, and finds that they just happen to be parked in front of the room numbered ten. Or, it would be ten, except the zero has rusted off, leaving nothing but an imprint of what was once there. " . . . it's this one."

"Oh, cool, less wheeling through flippin' gravel," Cass says.

"How much did it cost?" Rev asks, not leaving the van.

Shawna pauses. "She . . . didn't say," she says. Rev stops halfway through closing the door. She and Shawna stare at one another for a moment.

"Maybe she'll tell us when we check out?" Shawna says.

"Yeah, let's go with that," Cass says. "Now, could you help me out? I can't reach my chair from here."

Shawna gets it from the back and unfolds it, helping Cass down from the passenger's seat. Rev hasn't made a move.

"Come *on*," Cass says, "I'm *tired*."

Rev shakes her head, hugging herself.

Shawna reaches in and takes her arm, trying to pull her out. "It's going to be okay," she says.

Rev shakes her head more furiously this time, fighting Shawna's pull, trembling.

"Rev, you're being ridiculous," Shawna says, pulling harder.

"Just let her sleep in the van," Cass says with a yawn.

"No. We're going into the room. We need beds. We need decent sleep. It's fine." Shawna finally pulls Rev out of the van, both of them stumbling. Rev is looking around like a cornered animal, now holding Shawna's arm in a death grip. Shawna wraps her other arm around her and walks her forward. Cass grunts and forces her wheels through the gravel.

When they enter their room, Shawna tells herself

that it could have been much worse. The two beds have sheets, at least, though she's not willing to smell them to make sure that they're clean. There are no *visible* cockroaches hanging around the room, which is a plus, but a sour scent hangs in the air, smelling almost as sickly green as the walls. The TV's screen is shattered, but they weren't planning on watching whatever four channels this motel gets, anyway.

"You see?" Shawna says. "Fine." She tries to flick the lights on. They don't work.

Rev whimpers and squeezes her eyes shut.

"We just . . . " Shawna says, " . . . need to get to bed. It'll be better in the morning."

"Works for me," Cass says, wheeling forward. She lifts herself onto one of the beds.

"How are they?" Shawna asks.

"Uncomfortable," Cass says and falls asleep.

Shawna leads Rev to the other bed and climbs into it, not daring to pull the covers back, and cuddles up next to her. The sheets smell just as sour as she'd feared, and Shawna has the worst feeling that they haven't been washed in years.

She supposes that this is what happens when a fifteen-year-old is left to run an entire motel by herself, but she stops herself from judging the girl again. It's a bed to lie in. A non-moving, non-bumpy bed.

"I really don't like it here," Rev finally mutters, tightening her grip on Shawna.

"Shh. It's only for a few hours," Shawna says. "Try to get some sleep, okay? We'll be back on the road before you know it."

Rev whimpers a little more and curls into Shawna, but she's soon asleep, too.

Shawna is left awake. Something—be it the smell or the lack of electricity or the general creepiness of the place—will not let her sleep. When she's sure that Rev is asleep, she stands up and starts pacing, trying to figure out what isn't letting her relax. It takes almost an hour, but she finally narrows it down.

It's the girl at the desk, the supposed owner of this place, Cici. There's something that just isn't right about her. Something about the way she looked at Shawna, something about the way she said and did things refuses to sit right with her.

She glances down at her bandmates, sleeping in the darkness, making sure that they're alright before stepping into the cool summer night. She heads towards the front desk. The lights in the room are off, so she hesitates before trying the door. It's open. Cici had said that she would be there all night. She sees the book that Cici was reading earlier and can't make out the title in the darkness. It looks old, though. Not as old as the register, but still old. The small amount of light from the windows catches on a little bell, just off to the side. Shawna hovers her hand over it, then rings it.

Cici pops up from behind the desk. "Wha? Huh? Whossat?" she says, looking around wildly. Her hair is a bushy mess and her eyes are only half open. Shawna leans back to avoid the possibility of getting hit.

"Um, I was here earlier? You said to come talk to you if I needed anything?" she says.

Cici squints in the darkness and clicks on the desk

lamp. "Oh! It's you," she says, her expression morphing into a smile. "Shawna, right?"

"Yeah, how did you—?"

"You signed the register."

"Oh, yeah. That's right." Shawna raises her head a little to glance behind the desk and catches a glimpse of a pillow and blanket. "Were you sleeping back there?" she asks, pointing at them.

"What can I do for you?" Cici asks, talking over the end of Shawna's sentence.

"Oh, um, the electricity in our room isn't working," she says, electing to ignore the makeshift bed behind the desk.

"Sucks," Cici says with a chuckle.

Shawna pauses, unsure what to do with that. "So . . . can you fix it? Or something?" she asks.

Cici rests her elbow on the desk and her head on her hand and smiles up at Shawna. "Girl, there hasn't been electricity in this building since I started living here," she says.

Living here? That seems an odd way to put it.

"What about that?" Shawna points at the little lamp.

"Batteries," Cici says. She clicks it on and off a few times as Shawna watches.

On and off.

There's really something not right about all this.

On and off.

Shouldn't she be more worried about the fact that there's no electricity? Especially since she claims that she owns the place.

On and off.

Well, she never really did claim that, did she?

On.

"You don't own this motel, do you? You don't even work here."

"Well, obviously," Cici says. She smiles as if she's proud that Shawna's finally figured it out.

Shawna feels a mixture of fear and embarrassment swirl around in the pit of her stomach. How could she not have realized? It was obvious from the moment they pulled onto the gravel. She takes a step back from the desk.

"Then why did you . . . ? What was with all the . . . ?" She gestures to the desk with both hands, implying the whole show she'd put on earlier.

Cici shrugs. "I think you're cute. Wanted to help you out," she says.

Shawna pauses, her brow furrowing. "*Huh?*"

"It's a pretty good place to crash. Wanted to share that with you. Plus, if you pulled up to the motel with a clearly broken sign and decided to ignore the fact that there's a fifteen-year-old 'owner,' I figured you and your friends must be desperate."

Shawna wasn't sure if "desperate" was the word she'd use. This was simply the first motel they came across and they were all very tired. Shawna was *still* tired, but Rev was right. This place is sketchy beyond sketchy. Shawna considers just rousing her friends and getting the hell out of here, but thinks twice about it. Rev was nervous all day. She needs some decent rest, and she was never going to be able to wake Cass until Cass wanted to be woken.

She decides to let them sleep but, with all this new information, she doubts that *she'll* be able to. She looks at Cici. "Why are *you* crashing here?" she asks.

"Oh, you know. Because I'm a disappointment to my family." Her tone is nonchalant, but her fists clench and her "easy" smile is tight. "Probably better off here than there, anyway," she continues, forcing a laugh. "What about you?" She's reaching for a distraction, a change of subject, and Shawna is happy to oblige. If she can't sleep, she might as well talk.

"We're a band, actually. On our way to a gig." It feels so *good* to say that, like they're official. The perfect distraction.

"You're in a *band*?" Cici asks, smile widening and becoming more real. "Wow! That's so cool!" She props her head on her fists and stares at Shawna with eyes wide and full of wonder and adoration.

Shawna can't remember a time when anyone had looked at her like that. Ever. She feels heat creeping into her cheeks and a giddy smile spreading on her face. "Yeah, we're pretty awesome," she says, going to lean against the desk like she's cool. She forgets that she's taken a step back from it and her elbow slices through thin air, but she catches herself before she can fall. She takes a step forward, her elbow not missing the desk this time, and tries to pretend that didn't just happen.

Cici giggles.

Now that she's closer and less tense, Shawna starts to notice the dark brown of her eyes. So dark, it's almost black. Chapped lips crack to smile at Shawna and she smells like cheap public bathroom soap.

"What kind of music do you play?" Cici asks.

"Mostly rock 'n' roll," Shawna says, "with a little punk thrown in. You know. All that stuff."

"A punk rocker, huh?" Cici glances at her surroundings. "This might be a good experience for you, then."

Shawna laughs, but takes a glance around as well. Cracked glass and plaster, no electricity, no one else around. She remembers their song about running away, all the yearning in it, all the glory, the freedom. She feels none of that here.

"When's the gig?" Cici asks.

"Tomorrow night. In Indianapolis."

"Hey, that's not too far from here!"

"Yeah. We're trying to rest up a bit so we can put on our best performance."

"You should probably get back to your beauty sleep then," Cici says.

"Beauty sleep? I don't need beauty sleep! I'm already drop-dead gorgeous! Our band is the Beauty School Dropouts after all!" Shawna says.

Cici snorts. "Really? Like from *Grease*?"

Shawna smiles. Not many people get the reference. "Yeah!"

Cici starts to sing the song their band name is referencing, doing a little dance with it. Shawna giggles and joins her.

– – –

At some point, they end up on the roof of the van, lying on their backs and staring at the stars. They're just far enough from a major city for the stars to be more visible than what Shawna gets to see at home. Cici is resting her head on Shawna's chest and pointing out constellations. The poor girl is touch-starved and hasn't even seen another person in weeks. Shawna doesn't mind. She enjoys cuddles, and Cici's hair is fun to play with.

" . . . and there's the Big and Little Dippers, but they're also known as Ursa Major and Ursa Minor. The bears. There are a lot of legends about them. Ooo, and Leo! My favorite!"

"You know a lot about stars," Shawna says.

"I spend a lot of time in the library," Cici says. "Free information, warm place to stay for a while. It's nice. Plus, I got a good place to watch them from." She spreads her arms to indicate the sky above them.

Shawna had never thought of libraries like that, always associating them with homework and the local knitting circle (of which Cass is a secret member).

Then again, she'd always associated homelessness with drunks and stupidity, not clever, funny, young girls in need of a hug.

Could this be Shawna? If she ran away—*really* ran away—is Cici who she'd become?

Someone's feet crunch on the gravel and the girls sit up to see a man with no shirt walking up to the van with a crowbar. He's the skinniest person Shawna has ever seen, in a frightening way. His too-pale skin reflects the moonlight, which deepens the shadows cast by the outlines of his ribs. His arms are covered in dark splotches, shaking with the weight of the black bar in his hands. His eyes are wide and sunken, exaggerated by the bags under them. It looks more like a skeleton is walking towards them than a man.

"*Hey!*" Cici shouts. The man freezes. She lets a stream of Spanish loose on him, and he drops the bar and sprints away.

"*Crackheads,*" Cici says with disgust once he's gone and lies back down.

Shawna continues to stare in the direction he ran,

unsure. The night had been turning out so nice, but that half-dead man had startled her out of whatever spell Cici had put her under. They're squatting in an abandoned building. Their van could have been broken into. Their gear could have been stolen. *They* could have been attacked.

She needs to wake her bandmates up and leave. Now. She'll carry Cass into the van herself, if she has to.

"Shawna? What's wrong?" Cici asks, tugging at her arm.

"I have to go," Shawna says.

Cici sits back up.

"What? Why? I thought you guys had a few more hours until you had to leave," she says.

Shawna turns and looks at Cici. The fear and urgency in her eyes must be apparent, because Cici's expression falls.

"Oh. I see. Yeah. Dangerous place I live in and all that," Cici says, starting to climb off the top of the van. "Don't want to risk your safety."

"Cici, wait," Shawna says, following her.

"No, no. I get it. I know. I wouldn't be here, either, if I had a choice." It sounds more like a fact that she's been forced to accept rather than something she truly understands. There's an undertone of bitterness and hurt in her voice.

"I don't mean it like that." Does she? She's not sure. At this point, Shawna just wants to do something about the hurt in Cici's voice.

"No, you do," Cici says, turning to her. She doesn't sound angry or accusatory, just sad. She sighs.

"I'm not asking you to stay," she says. "I'm . . . I don't know what I'm asking. I don't know if I'm asking anything, at all. It's just . . . it sucks, living like this. It really sucks." She hugs herself and looks away.

Shawna isn't sure what to say to that, so she pulls Cici into a hug. It takes a moment, but Cici melts into the contact, hugging Shawna back.

"I'm sorry," Shawna says.

"It's not like it's your fault," Cici mumbles into her shoulder. "My parents kicked me out. I'm just too stubborn to apologize for whatever I did. Thought it might be better to be away from all the shouting and screaming and my dad . . . " She shudders. "But it just sucks in different ways. I just . . . I can't. I can't go back now . . . "

Shawna's heart aches for this girl. There has to be *something* she can do. "Maybe . . . you can come stay with me?" She's not sure of the offer, but it's all she's got.

Cici shakes her head. "I'll only slow you guys down. Live-in groupies are bad for business."

"No. No, I mean when the gig is over. When I go home . . . " Because, if the billion-and-two messages on her phone are any indication, she can still go home. She can always go home to a pair of loving parents who she knows will never, ever kick her out. She can go home right now, if she wanted.

Cici can't.

"No," Cici says, "I don't want to get between you and your parents. Just . . . I'll be fine. Really. I'll be okay."

Shawna's not so sure about that, but she doesn't push it. She just holds the girl.

– – –

Not long after, the bandmates are all in the car again and Shawna is asleep in the passenger's seat.

Cass stares at her, having woken up in confusion after an hour of Rev driving. "So Shawna let us stay in what was probably some kinda crack house?" she says.

"I mean, that's kind of a crude way to put it, but I guess?" Rev says.

"Insane. She's insane. I'm going back to sleep." She shifts in her seat and does so.

Chapter Nine

THE MUSIC IS DOWN TO A SOFT WHISPER FROM THE speakers as Shawna and Cass sleep. Rev is still driving or, at least, she should be.

Rev is not in the driver's seat. She's on the side of the road, desperately looking between a map and the highway sign that had caused her to stop the car. Something isn't right. Something is off. A letter here or there, a number with too many digits. This would be so much easier with Google Maps, but if she turns on her phone now—or any of their phones—she's going to have a panic attack at the sheer amount of messages. She can't drive with a panic attack, so here she is, in the dark with a paper map, trying to convince herself that she's wrong. She *has* to be on the right road, she just *has* to.

Part of her has already accepted that she's not. They should have been at the Angry Whirlpool hours ago.

A car with only one working headlight drives past, then slows and comes to a stop in front of the van. Rev freezes, not sure what to do or think, her tight grip crumpling the sides of the map.

A woman steps out. A large woman. A mountainous woman. Rev has to crane her neck to look up at her as she walks closer. She finds herself rooted to the spot, unable to say or do anything other than stare.

The woman glances over at the van, then gives Rev a once-over.

"You lost or somethin'?" she asks, single eyebrow raised, hands on her hips, thick southern accent dripping from her words.

Rev is unable to speak. What if she says that she's lost? Would this woman do something? Lead her somewhere she doesn't want to go? Would she help?

Is Rev even lost? She isn't sure. She's clutching the map to her chest.

"You gonna say somethin', kid?" the woman asks after a few more moments of Rev's silence.

Rev takes a sharp breath, then looks down at the map, then at the road, then into the distance. Anywhere but at the woman. "Oh . . . w-well . . . I-I mean . . . I just . . . I mean . . . "

As Rev goes on, the woman's brow furrows. She glances in the direction Rev is staring off into, then turns back to Rev. "Ya sound a bit nervous, there, girlie," she says.

"U-um . . . " Rev says. Nervous doesn't begin to describe what she's feeling.

The woman sighs. "I'm not gonna eat ya or any-thin'," she says, "I just wanna help. Honest. Ain't safe for a young girl on the side of the road at night."

Rev is aware of this. Hyper-aware, in fact. She looks down at the now-crumpled map, then back up at the woman. No words come to her.

"Just . . . nod if you think you're lost," the woman tries.

"If you think you're *what*?" Rev and the woman turn at the sound of Cass's voice. She's awake and staring at Rev.

"Who's this, then?" the woman asks, raising an eyebrow again. Rev wonders how she's able to do that, mostly to avoid the rage pouring off of Cass, to refocus her mind on anything but the fear trying to fill it.

"Nobody," Cass snaps at the woman. "But *you*"— she points at Rev—"I am going to *kill* you!"

"What's going on?" Shawna asks, halfway through a yawn.

"Oh, Shawna!" Cass says in the most obviously fake pleasant tone anyone has ever used. "So glad you're awake! Sleep well?"

Shawna blinks a few times, taking in her surroundings. "Why are we stopped? Did something happen to the engine?" she asks.

Cass releases a loud, long, and very fake laugh. "See,

the funny thing is, *apparently*, we're *lost*!" She returns to glaring at Rev.

"Lost?" Shawna takes a moment to process this. She turns to Rev then, concern written all over her face. "Rev?"

Rev looks away from her bandmates, crumpling the map to her chest again. The woman puts a rough hand on her shoulder. She flinches. The woman removes her hand, and Rev takes the breath that had caught in her throat.

"Now, don't be too hard on your friend, here," the woman says.

"Give me a reason, lady," Cass says. She looks ready to drag herself through the window and slam her fists into whatever part of Rev she can reach.

Again, the woman raises an eyebrow. "Folks make mistakes," she says. She turns to Rev. "Lemme see that map a' yours, hon."

Rev hands it to her.

The woman smooths it out and holds it so that

both she and Rev can see. "Where y'all tryin' to get to?" she asks.

"Indianapolis," Shawna says, getting out of the car to look at the map with them.

The woman squints at the map, then looks up at the road. "Which way were you headin'?" she asks.

Rev points out which was she was going.

"Ooo, that is the wrong direction, girlie," the woman says.

"*Wrong direction*?" Cass says. "Where the hell are we right now?"

The woman scans the map for a moment and points.

"Looks like we're somewhere around Minneapolis, Minnesota," Shawna says.

"Minne . . . ? We're should be, like *there* right now!" Cass says.

"I'm sure we can still make it . . . " Shawna says, rubbing her eyes, not sounding sure at all. "We still have . . . " She counts on her fingers. "Ten hours before we have to get there?"

"'S about a nine-hour drive," the woman says.

Cass unleashes a noise somewhere between a growl and a scream. "I'M GONNA *KILL* YOU, REV!" she shouts.

"I made a mistake!" Rev shouts back, raising the map to hide herself. She wishes she could just fight with Cass like she normally does. "I'm sorry!"

"Not as sorry as you're about to be!" Cass shouts.

"*Shut up!*" Shawna shouts.

Cass and Rev pause and turn to her, surprised.

"Both of you just shut up for two seconds! God, I'm so sick of this! We're doing this thing! We said we were doing this! We're not gonna kill each other before we can! We're gonna get back in the van, we're gonna keep driving, and you're both going to stop yelling at each other!" She stops to take a few shaky breaths. "Please," she adds, voice breaking halfway through the word.

"Okay, Shawna," Rev says, concerned.

"Yeah," Cass says. She scrambles into the driver's seat. Rev knows she's not going to trust her to drive, and she's not sure Shawna should, either. Rev gets into the back seat.

Shawna sniffles and wipes away a tear that managed to escape.

"Everythin' alright between you three?" the woman asks.

"*Yes*, we're *fine*," Shawna snaps, then pauses. "I'm sorry," she says in a quieter tone. "Thank you for your help. You've been very kind to us." She shakes the woman's hand.

"Y'all take care of yourselves, now," the woman says, giving Shawna's hand a small squeeze, "and each other. Be safe, okay?"

Shawna nods, then climbs into the passenger's seat and stares out the window, trying to hold back the rest of the tears.

"I really am sorry," Rev mutters from the back seat.

"Just shut up, Rev," Shawna says.

Rev flinches and curls into herself. She counts her breaths. It's going to be fine. Everything's going to be fine . . .

Isn't it?

She loses count and starts over again.

Chapter Ten

"Hey, Shawna?" says Cass an hour into driving

"What is it, Cass?" Shawna is exhausted, emotionally and physically. She couldn't get any sleep after the incident on the side of the road and spent most of the time trying to convince herself that she wasn't about to cry. Nine hours until the gig . . .

"I think we need to talk about Rev."

Shawna groans a little. "I honestly don't want to hear it. Really, whatever annoyance or problem or grudge you have, I just don't want to hear it."

"It's important."

Shawna scoffs.

"No, I mean it. Don't you think it's a little weird that, twice now, she's held us up?"

Shawna glances into the back seat, making sure that Rev is still asleep. She turns back to Cass. "What do you mean?" she asks.

"I mean there's no way she just 'forgot' her guitar. And getting us lost? She was driving the *wrong way*. *Backwards*, Shawna. Seven and a half hours backwards."

"Are you . . . are you trying to say that she's *sabotaging* us?"

"Finally seeing the pattern, are we?"

"No way. Rev wouldn't do that. She's our *friend*, Cass."

"She's *your* friend," Cass says. "Ever noticed how we don't get along? Like, at all?"

"No. I never noticed that," Shawna says in a flat, sarcastic tone. "Friends fight. There are plenty of times when I've seen you two get along fine."

"What about the charity gig, huh? Remember what she said about that? She said that we shouldn't do it."

"I mean, we weren't getting *paid*," Shawna says. "She was probably just worried about us being taken advantage of. Or maybe she was just nervous."

"*Listen* to yourself! You're just trying to defend her and not looking at facts. She doesn't want to be a part of this. She never did. The only reason that she's here is because you forced her into it."

"No. No, that's not true."

"It is and you know it. It's what you *do*, Shawna."

Shawna thinks about that, thinks back to middle school, when she first had the idea for the band. She thinks about the moment she asked Rev to start a band with her. She caught Rev singing something and asked her what it was. She had to push and cajole before Rev even admitted that she had written it herself, and it took months of begging and needling and convincing until Rev agreed to start the band on the condition that she didn't have to sing. How much of that was Shawna forcing herself and her own ideas onto Rev?

Maybe talking about how she couldn't play an instrument was Rev's way of trying to back out without hurting Shawna's feelings, but Shawna got her an electric guitar and a "How to Play" book and insisted that she learn. She didn't even consider Rev's feelings, and when she did, maybe she was reading them wrong. Maybe it wasn't sentiment that made Rev push against Cass joining, but another escape attempt.

Shawna always thought that her nudging and pushing made Rev's life better, that her friend was happier for it. What if that wasn't the case? What if she was wrong this whole time? Cass was immediately enthusiastic about the endeavor, but Rev always hung back about everything. Even the nickname "Rev" took a long time and a lot of insisting from Shawna for her to accept.

"I still don't believe it," Shawna says, not even convincing herself.

"She's dead weight," Cass says. "If we ever want this band to go anywhere, we gotta ditch her."

Shawna doesn't answer for a moment.

"Fine, then."

Shawna freezes. That voice wasn't hers or Cass's. She turns back to see Rev glaring at them.

"Rev, I—" Shawna tries to say.

"Pull the van over," Rev interrupts her.

"Rev, don't be so—" Cass tries to say.

"I said, pull the van over!" Rev shouts over her.

Cass finally does just before they enter a small town. Rev practically kicks the door open and slams it shut behind her. She starts marching away, taking nothing with her.

Shawna scrambles out of the van after her. "Rev! No, don't go!"

"Why?" Rev snaps, turning to face her. "Why shouldn't I go? I'm just dead weight, right? And you"—she points at Cass—"never liked me! So why should I stick around?"

"You're being ridiculous," Cass says, rolling her eyes.

"You can go screw yourself, Cass! You both can! I'm leaving." She turns around again and continues to walk.

"Rev, please, it's not like that!" Shawna runs up and grabs Rev's arm.

"Stop trying to *convince* me of things!" Rev says, jerking her arm away, "You're not always right! Sometimes, you're just delusional!" She keeps walking.

Shawna isn't sure what to do or say. It feels like the world as she knows is has been torn apart. She's doubting her instinct, which is to run after Rev and convince her to stay. She hesitates and questions herself long enough to lose sight of the girl she thought was her best friend.

"Good riddance, then!" Cass shouts after her.

Shawna clenches her fists and turns on Cass. After all this time, the tears have finally taken over. "What is *wrong* with you?" she says.

"What's wrong with *me*?" Cass spits back.

"You couldn't have *at least* waited until she was somewhere she couldn't hear you? Or until after the show? Or not said it at all because it was *awful* and *mean*?"

"It was the truth!" Cass is shouting now. "She hates

this band! She hates me! She hates you! She doesn't want us to be able to *do* anything because she's stupid and pathetic and worthless, and she wants everyone else to feel like she does!" Cass is crying now, too. Shawna has never seen her cry before. She feels like she should care and try to comfort her, but she's too upset. Things have gone too far for her to stop now.

"Well, why don't you go do something on your own, then!" Shawna shouts. "Go ahead and drive away and be your own band! I'm going to go find my friend." She turns and runs after Rev.

Chapter Eleven

SHAWNA RUNS INTO EVERY STORE AND STOPS EVERY pedestrian she finds, asking about Rev. The small town gives her more places to hide than if she had just been walking down the highway. What if something happens to her? What if someone kidnaps her or hurts her, or something worse? It would be all Shawna's fault for even thinking that way about her friend, for letting Cas say things like that, for pushing Rev past what she was comfortable with. Rev has been like the sister she never had. Sisters don't do this to one another, do they?

Finally, Shawna finds her in the corner booth of a

ma-and-pa diner, head buried in her arms on the table. She lets out a breath, glad that Rev is at least safe, and works on building up the courage to walk up to her.

"Rev?" Shawna says once she enters the diner.

No answer.

"Rev, I'm so sorry. I didn't . . . I didn't want any of this to happen."

Rev lets out an audible sob, and Shawna notices that her shoulders are shaking.

"Rev?" One of her hands hovers over Rev's back, hesitating to touch her.

"I'm sorry I said all that stuff to you," Rev says, the words muffled by her arms and her tears. "Do you hate me?"

"No!" Shawna wraps her arms around her best friend who, despite everything, seems to still be her best friend. "I could never hate you. Never, never, never!"

Rev turns into the hug, wrapping her arms around Shawna, as well. She buries her face in her shoulder, breath hitching on sobs. Shawna buries her face in

Rev's shoulder, in turn. She can feel the tears in her eyes, but doesn't let herself cry this time.

"Do you think Cass hates me?" Rev asks after a few minutes.

"Cass . . . I think Cass had her own issues to sort out," Shawna says.

"She was right, though," Rev mutters.

Shawna pulls away, concern and unease hitting her again. "What?"

"This always happens," Rev says, not looking up at Shawna. "Every time something fun comes up or something that I want to do happens, I always just . . . I don't know."

"I don't understand," Shawna says, shaking her head. Is she saying that she still wants to do this or that she's sabotaging them? Or both?

"I don't either!" Rev says, looking up. "I'm just . . . I'm so *scared*. All the time. Sometimes, I don't even know *what* it is I'm scared of, I just know that I'm scared. Making plans with friends is unsettling enough, but big things like this? Joining a band, running away to go to a gig? It's terrifying. It's like . . . a part of my mind knows that I really want to go and do these things, but a bigger part is just crushing that down and telling me I should stay at home, where nothing bad can happen."

"But nothing *good* can happen, then, either."

"I know! But it's like it doesn't matter if it's good or bad. So long as I stay at home, I can just . . . not have to worry about it. I make a lot of excuses. And convince myself that they're *rational* excuses. Like, 'I can't play an instrument, so I can't join the band' or 'I forgot my guitar at home.' It's like I'm just sabotaging myself, and it's just . . . it's awful 'cause I always, *always* regret it, no matter how many times I tell myself I don't."

Shawna pulls her into another hug.

"Why didn't you tell me?" she asks.

"Because it's stupid," Rev mutters into Shawna's shoulder. "It's stupid and pathetic."

"No, no it's not that." Shawna squeezes her a little

tighter. "It sounds a lot like anxiety and stuff, you know?"

Rev nods. "I . . . I usually take, like, medicine for it . . . " she admits.

"Did you bring any with you?"

Rev's breath hitches on another sob.

Shawna takes that as a "no." "That, um, that's probably not good," she says.

Rev mutters something ending in "stupid."

"You're not stupid, Rev. You're my best friend, and I don't make friends with stupid people."

Rev lets out something between a chuckle and a sob.

"Seriously, girl, I love you. You're dealing with some tough stuff, but it's okay. And, I mean, you got this far! Like, you started the band with me! We did that charity gig! That was fun! And we drove all the way out here, and you came with us! You didn't just stay at home."

Rev sniffles. "Yeah. I guess," she says.

"Yeah! You're awesome! And you did all that even

with that whole big part of your brain telling you not to. You kicked its butt!"

"This time . . . " Rev mumbles.

Shawna pauses. "Yeah, we should really get those meds back. But still! Let's take the win."

"But I still didn't bring my guitar. And I got us lost. And lost us time . . . "

"Yeah, but Cass is driving now, and she drives like a maniac on a *good* day."

Rev chuckles, then frowns. "I can't face her," she says.

"You totally can. I'll help. If this . . . if the Beauty School Dropouts are going to end up going down, I—*we*—can't let it end like this. Besides, we left all our stuff in the van."

Rev chuckles again. She squeezes Shawna a little tighter and Shawna squeezes back.

"I love you so much," Rev says.

"I love you, too," Shawna says.

– – –

Cass is sitting alone in the van, wiping away angry tears. She has the steering wheel in one hand, her grip vice-like. Her other hand is on the gas. All she needs to do is hit it and keep moving, go and do her own thing, like Shawna said.

She doesn't need those girls. She *doesn't*. She can do things on her own. She doesn't need to be wheeled around like some invalid. She doesn't need anyone.

Rev never liked her, anyway. She was always arguing and making a fuss about things. Cass was right to say that she was dragging them down.

She doesn't need Rev.

And Shawna probably only wanted her in the band out of pity. Cass is the only one in their high school with such a visible disability, after all. She wouldn't have asked her, otherwise. There's no other possible reason. Cass hates being pitied.

She doesn't need Shawna, either.

She can make it fine without those two. Even though Rev is the only person willing to fight with her like an equal. Even though she knows Shawna heard her playing in the band room, first. Even though both girls back off when Cass tells them to and help when Cass needs them to. Even though Shawna has hip-checked people who've grabbed the back of her wheelchair more than once. Even though she loves arguing with Rev and loves every piece of music Rev writes and loves that she makes sure they each get a spotlight in every song. Even though she loves Shawna's attitude and ambition and excitement. Even though they're the only friends she's ever had.

She doesn't need them.

She screams and slams her fists on the steering wheel, making the car's horn scream along with her.

She doesn't need them.

She *doesn't.*

SHE DOESN'T!

She starts to cry again because the van they all learned to drive together feels empty. She wants to throw something or punch something, but she just keeps crying. She got along fine without friends before she met Rev and Shawna, so why does it feel so important that they're around now? Why can't she just hit the gas and drive off? They're both idiots! Idiots!

Cass is an idiot.

She hits the gas and starts driving in the direction she saw Rev and Shawna go, glaring out the windshield.

She hates them.

She loves them.

She hates that she loves them.

She slows down and searches the town for signs of her two stupid best friends.

– – –

Rev and Shawna jump when they hear a car horn blare as they walk out of the little diner. They're so startled, they nearly drop the greasiest sandwiches they have ever seen in their lives (apparently, Ma and Pa don't take kindly to loiterers and insisted that the girls buy something). They look up and see Cass parked on the side of the road, glaring at them out the driver's side window.

"You two gonna climb in or what? We've only got eight hours to get there and two whole states to cross," Cass says, looking away from the girls.

Rev and Shawna look at one another, then head over to the van. Rev climbs into the passenger's seat and hands Cass a sandwich, looking down at her own. Shawna leans over from the back seat, looking between the two in concern.

Cass looks down at the sandwich, then picks it up and starts picking at the tape holding the wrapping on. "I'm sorry," she says, focusing fully on the sandwich. "I . . . shouldn't have said all that stuff about you. You're an important part of the band. You do a lot."

"I'm sorry I ran off," Rev says, also focusing on her sandwich, tossing it between her hands, "and that I caused so many delays."

"Yeah, well, stupid stuff happens." Cass lowers her voice and stops picking at the tape, but doesn't look up. "And I'd rather deal with your stupid stuff than anyone else's, I guess."

Rev looks up from her sandwich, a small smile on her face.

Shawna reaches over the back of the seats and pulls them both into a hug. "I love you guys! I really, really do!" she says.

"We love you too, Shawna," Rev says with a little chuckle.

"Get off!" Cass says.

"Not until you say you love me!" Shawna says, a hint of a smirk hiding in her expression.

"I'll die first!" Cass says.

"Oh, just say you love her, you stubborn jerk," Rev says, the smile not fading from her face.

"Oh, *fine. I love you.* Happy?" Cass says.

"Yes!" Shawna gives her a big, loud kiss on the cheek.

"Disgusting!" Cass says, pulling away, but a smile is starting to creep across her face.

Shawna and Rev both laugh.

Cass finally rips open the sandwich paper, forgetting the tape. She tears a bite out of it and things feel like they're back to the way they're supposed to be.

Chapter Twelve

SHAWNA TAPS HER FOOT ANXIOUSLY, FEELING LIKE there isn't time to be filling up the gas tank. Cass taps the steering wheel in tandem, eager to get going. Rev went inside to get snacks for everyone.

"Is that thing working yet?" Cass asks.

"I've pressed the button twenty times, and it still hasn't started!" Shawna says.

Cass groans and bangs her head against the steering wheel. "The universe is plotting against us."

"It's going to work," Shawna says, pressing the button again. It beeps and refuses to pump gas.

"Hey guys," Rev says, walking back, carrying two bags. "We all filled up?"

Both Cass and Shawna groan.

"What's wrong?" Rev asks.

"It won't. Fill. Up," Cass says, punctuating each pause with a bang of her head on the steering wheel. Shawna hits the button again and, again, it does nothing.

Cass slams on the horn, making Shawna and Rev jump. "Hey! Give someone else a chance, will ya!" she shouts at the person filling up in front of them. There are only two pumps at this station, and the guy in front of them has spent the entire time on his phone and not filling up his tank. He throws a rude hand gesture their way without taking his focus off of his phone.

"I'm going to *murder* him," Cass says, gripping the steering wheel.

"I'm gonna go talk to whoever is in that store," Shawna says. She walks in, leaving Rev to climb into the van and Cass to glare at her newfound enemy.

"Excuse me?" Shawna asks the cashier.

"What can I do you for?" she asks. She's an older woman. Her name tag says "Irma" and her smile is kind, if missing a few teeth.

"I was just wondering if you know what's up with the second pump out there? It's not really working for us."

Irma looks out the window at the pump Shawna indicated and her smile turns apologetic. "Honey, those pumps ain't worked in ten years," she says.

"Come again?"

"They're dead. Been dead a long time. I'm really sorry."

Shawna is taken aback by this new information. She just can't accept it. It's not possible that they've gotten this far, through all the delays and emotional turmoil, only to be stopped by a lack of gas.

"Where's the . . . where's the next pump?" Shawna asks, sounding almost in a daze.

"Bout . . . twenty miles from here?" Irma says.

"T-twe—" She can't bring herself to say the rest of the number. There is no way the van is going to make it that far. "Any other place we can get gas? Anywhere at all?"

"Not that I know of."

"But there *has* to be!"

"I'm sorry. There's just not." Irma looks out the window again. "Maybe you can ask Cal for help." She indicates the man at the other gas pump.

Shawna's shoulders slump. This man might be the last person they can get gas from in the next twenty miles, and Cass has already made an enemy of him. Just their luck.

She starts walking out, dejected. "Thanks," she murmurs as she pushes the door open.

"Sorry I couldn't be more help," Irma says.

Shawna tries to think of the positives of this interaction. The cashier was nice and seemed willing to help them out. She knows the man by name, which means he's a regular. If she and her friends can't convince him to help them out, maybe she can recruit the cashier to.

"Well?" Rev asks, looking at her nervously.

"The pumps don't work," Shawna says.

Cass lets out a string of expletives, punching the steering wheel a few times.

"Calm down! What did that steering wheel ever do to you?" Rev says, sounding just as tense if not as furious.

"Don't test me right now!" Cass shouts.

"*However*," Shawna says, trying to break into the tension, "Cal, over there, might be able to help us. Maybe." She nods at the man, whose attention has not moved from his phone once.

Cass pauses banging her head against the wheel to stare up at the man, her jaw hanging open. "You've got to be kidding me," she says.

"We don't have a lot of options, Cass," Shawna says.

"You've *got* to be kidding me!"

"I don't think he's gonna accept an apology, I really don't," Rev says, shaking a little. "He seemed pretty upset about the horn thing and the shouting, and he's a strange guy at some random gas station and—"

Shawna reaches through the window and takes Rev's hand.

"We've got to try, Rev, we've got to. Me and Cass, we're both here for you, but it's time to *Rev it up* again," she says.

Rev looks into her eyes and squeezes her hand. "Okay," she says, still sounding nervous. "Okay, yeah. We gotta try. We've come this far."

"You don't even have to leave the van."

Rev nods, squeezing her eyes shut, obviously trying to control her breathing.

Cass takes a few deep breaths, as well. "I'm gonna have to apologize, aren't I?" she asks.

"Yeah," Shawna says.

Cass slams her head on the steering wheel one more time, causing Rev to flinch, then takes a few more deep breaths.

"A concussion isn't going to get you out of this," Shawna says.

"Just shut up and give me a minute," Cass says.

"I'll just go . . . butter him up," Shawna says, then

shudders at her own wording. That did not sound right, at all, but she walks forward, prepared for the buttering.

"Excuse me, sir?" she says.

Cal glances at her, then back down at his phone. "What?"

Shawna wonders what he's doing on there that's so important. "My friends and I happen to be a little stuck. You see, we're out of gas, and there isn't another station for twenty miles or so. I was wondering if, maybe, you'd be willing to help us out a little?" she asks.

Cal glances up at the van, where Rev and Cass quickly avert their stares, then back to Shawna.

"Why should I help a group of rude folks like yourselves?" he asks. There's a smug undertone in his speech making it hard for Shawna to keep up her friendly smile.

"My friend can apologize for shouting at you. We're all just a little stressed. You see, we're kind of on a deadline here and we really, really need to get to where we're going—fast," Shawna says.

Cal contemplates her. "Apologies don't buy gasoline," he says.

"We have money," Shawna says. "We'll pay you back."

The man smirks. "Dollars don't buy my interest," he says.

Shawna tenses. They're losing precious driving time and whatever would buy his interest doesn't sound very pleasant. She almost doesn't want to ask, but they're desperate. "What *would* buy your interest?"

The man glances around the station, he spots something, and the smirk is back on his face. "See that telephone pole up there? I want your rude friend to climb it and shout an apology down at me. Then, *maybe*, I'll let you have some of my gas," he says.

Shawna cranes her neck to see the top of the pole. She wouldn't climb that thing, even if she wanted to. It's dangerous, way too easy to fall and break your neck, or touch the wrong thing and get electrocuted.

"But . . . she can't," Shawna says, still staring up at the top of the pole.

"Then I guess you can't drive anywhere," Cal says, looking back down at his phone. Shawna can hear little beeps and dings that sound like some kind of game. He smirks at the screen. *He's playing a stupid game.* Shawna can feel something angry start to come to her throat.

The bell on top of the shop door tinkles.

"Calvin!" Irma shouts from the steps.

Cal's eyes go wide and he fumbles with his phone, catching it just in time with a look of horror at how close it was to shattering on the ground. Shawna can practically feel Cass's satisfied smirk from here.

"Are you being cruel, again?" Irma asks, hands on her hips, glaring at Cal.

Cal puffs out his chest and glares back. "They were being rude. Figured I'd teach 'em a lesson," he says.

"Oh, boo hoo!" Irma says, stepping down and marching up to Cal, "What kinda man are you? Tormentin' these poor, stranded little girls?"

"Listen, here, woman—" Cal says, pointing his phone at her.

Irma plucks it out of his fingers. "Don't you 'woman' me, boy! I oughta call your mother and ask her if you talk to her like that. Maybe tell her how you're treatin' these kids, on top of it."

Cal seems taken aback by this, unsure of what to say. "I'm . . . I'm a grown man! You can't threaten to call my mother on me!"

"Oh, can't I?" Irma opens his phone without a problem and shows him his mother's contact number. Her finger hovers over the dial button.

Cal's wide, angry, unsure eyes glance between the cashier, the phone, and the van a few times before he grunts and pulls a gas carton and a hose out of the back of his pickup.

A few minutes later, the van has enough gas to at least get them to the next station and Cal is leaning against his pickup, grumbling.

"You three drive safe, now," Irma says to them.

"And don't think too badly on Cal, here. He's really not as much of a jerk as he pretends to be."

Cal lets out an annoyed grunt and Cass gives him a flat look. "Seems like a pretty solid jerk to me," she says.

"I know." Irma shakes her head, then jerks it up. "Oh! There's something you ought to know before you head out. They're callin' for a big storm this afternoon, and these highways are kinda narrow."

"Probably shouldn't be driving," Cal mutters just loud enough for them to hear him.

"Yeah, you probably shouldn't, but you seem like you're in a hurry," Irma says.

"We are," Cass says, tapping her fingers against the steering wheel. She pauses and takes another deep breath. "Thank you for the gas and the warning," she says. Rev and Shawna stare at her with wide eyes.

"Any time," Irma says. "Get going now! Maybe you can outdrive the storm, but remember that wherever you're headin' ain't worth your lives."

"Right. Of course," Shawna says, recovering from her shock. "Thanks again!"

Irma waves as they drive off, elbowing Cal so that he waves too.

Chapter Thirteen

CASS HAS THE WINDSHIELD WIPERS WORKING SO FAST that Rev is afraid they'll fall off. She can hardly see anything out the side windows, and anything visible in the front window is soon distorted by what amounts to another three buckets of water tossed onto the windshield.

"Are you sure we shouldn't pull over? This seems like a little much to be driving through," Rev says.

"It'll be fine," Cass says.

"There's no other cars on the road, anyway," Shawna says.

"Yeah, because they're all smart enough not to drive in a storm like this!" Rev says.

"Stop it," Cass says, glaring at the road ahead. Or maybe she's trying to squint through the rain.

Rev can feel a lump in her throat. She doesn't know if that means she's going to cry or have a panic attack or both. She wants to get out of this car. She closes her eyes and tries to pretend that it's not happening, that they're not going to crash.

But they are . . .

No! They're not, no . . .

They are . . .

She feels Shawna take her hand. "Hey, it's gonna be okay, alright? I'm here. We're safe. It's okay," she says.

"No, it's not, we're not safe, it's not okay," Rev says, shaking her head.

"I said, stop it!" Cass says, gripping the wheel tightly. Rev knows that freaking out in the back seat probably isn't helping Cass's concentration, but she can't stop.

"Shhhh." Shawna is trying to comfort her, but it's

not helping. She needs to get out of this van. *She needs to get out!*

Then the van swerves, slipping on a large puddle in the road. Cass's eyes go wide and she grips the steering wheel even tighter than before, trying to keep control. Rev screams.

‒ ‒ ‒

The van stops on a muddy patch of grass just off the road. It didn't roll or crash into anything, and neither the equipment nor the band seem to be broken.

Rev is gasping and sobbing in the back. Cass is breathing heavily, frozen at the wheel, eyes still wide. Shawna looks at them both and feels a calm wash over her. Her friends are scared. She needs to help. She unbuckles and climbs into the back with Rev, unbuckling her, too, and taking hold of her shoulders.

"It's okay, Rev. It's okay, it's over. We're not hurt. You're not hurt. Everything's okay." Shawna repeats it like a mantra until Rev's breathing returns to normal, then slowly pulls her into a hug and lets her cry it out. That's one down.

Shawna turns to see that Cass is still in the same position. "Cass? Are you okay?" she asks, still hugging Rev.

"Huh? Um . . . I . . . uh-huh . . . " Cass says, not sounding sure.

"You did a really great job," Shawna says. "You kept control of the van and we're all okay, now."

"Yeah. Y-yeah. I did. I did that," Cass says. Her grip on the wheel begins to relax and her breathing slows back to normal.

Shawna puts a hand on her shoulder, keeping one arm around Rev. "We're all okay," she says.

Cass reaches over to grab her hand.

A tapping on the side of the van causes all three of the bandmates to jump. They sit in silence as it moves its way towards the driver's side door, then jump again when it knocks. Who could or would be out in this storm on the side of the road? Shawna can see a distorted shadow through the window, but that's about it. It knocks again.

"Is everyone alright in there?" says a muffled voice from outside.

When Cass rolls down the window, the bandmates are met with the face of a little old woman in a heavy, green rain jacket and dark sunglasses. She's holding a white cane.

"Is that a window I heard? Are you alright in there?" the woman asks.

"Yeah. Yeah, we're fine," Shawna says, recovering first.

"Are you *crazy*, lady?" Cass says. "What are you doin' out here in all this?"

"I should be asking you the same question," the woman says. "It's dangerous to be driving in a storm like this."

"Where . . . where did you *come* from?" Shawna asks. Rev is still crying in her arms. It feels like she's trying to burrow into Shawna's chest to escape this strange woman.

The woman points her cane at a small, green house just off the road. "I heard tires screeching and came out. Thought you might need some help," she says, then taps the top of the van with her cane. "Your car seems to be upright, though, which is good. You know why they call cars like these SUVs?"

"Why?" Shawna asks.

"Because they're Semi-Upright Vehicles."

Rev's sobbing turns into semi-hysterical laughter. Shawna realizes that she's joined in. Even Cass is shaking with stifled laughter. The joke isn't even that funny, but they all laugh until there are tears in their eyes (or, in Rev's case, *more* tears). They laugh and hug one another, and the woman waits patiently as they regain control of themselves, a little smile on her face.

"Would you like to come inside for a little bit? Wait out the worst of this storm?" the woman asks.

"No," Shawna says, a huge smile on her face. "No, sorry. Thanks for the offer, but we've got a gig to play in a few hours." For the first time in what feels like forever, she's excited as she says it. She's not stressed or worried about getting there on time. She still wants to, still wants to feel that crowd loving her, but if they can't make it, if the storm really does keep them from it, it won't matter. What will matter is that they survived, that they stayed together. There will be more opportunities, but even if there aren't, everything they've gone through will still have been worth it. She looks into Rev's and Cass's eyes and she knows that they feel the same. They're going to see this to its end, no matter what that end is. And they're going to do it together.

"A gig, huh?" the woman says. "Well, I'm sure you'll do wonderfully."

"Thanks," Shawna says with a giggle.

"If you're gonna keep going through this storm, though, you'll have to drive more carefully. You're not out of the woods, yet."

Shawna feels something odd settle in her stomach when the woman says that, like she's talking about more than just driving on slick roads. She doesn't know where the feeling came from or what it means, but it gives her pause. They've been through so much already, but maybe they're not quite finished yet.

"Alright, lady, we'll be careful," Cass says.

"Thanks for worrying about us," Rev mutters, a small smile on her face.

"It's not a problem, dears," the woman says.

She walks away, tapping her cane in front of her, as Cass pulls back into the road, but Shawna watches her until she can't see the little green coat or the little green house anymore.

– – –

For the next couple of hours, Cass drives slower and more carefully. Rev is back to strumming on her acoustic, her eyes closed, trying to keep herself from panicking again.

Shawna is still staring out the window, thinking about the old lady. "You didn't feel it, at all?" she asks Cass sometime after the storm lets up. They discussed Shawna's strange feeling earlier, and Cass said

Shawna was just being weird and on edge from the near-accident.

"Are you seriously still on about this?" Cass asks, rolling her eyes.

"I can't help it," Shawna says. "It's a gut feeling, Cass. I trust my gut."

"Since when?"

Shawna huffs and turns back to the window. She pulls her phone out of her pocket. The screen is black. She'd turned her phone back off after she'd used it to find a guitar store. It was too stressful, and the million messages used up too much of her battery. She moves her thumb to the power button.

"Don't do it," Cass says. "You're gonna regret it. We're supposed to be getting pumped for the show right now! Aren't you pumped? I'm pumped! Aren't you pumped, Rev?"

"Yeah, I'm pumped!" Rev says.

"Yeah!" Cass says. "So, seriously, put that thing away."

Shawna considers it, then holds her thumb down

on the power button. The screen lights up and the little opening chime rings out. As soon as it warms up, her screen is bombarded with notifications. Emails, Facebook messages, texts, calls, the whole nine yards. Her brow furrows and she hisses a little, as if she's been physically struck.

Rev is playing a little louder in the back seat, and Cass lets out a disappointed sigh. Shawna unlocks her phone and scrolls through the most recent messages. They're all from her dads. Some are long, some are short, some are worried, some are angry, but most are whr r u? Her heart breaks for them. They're her parents. They love her, she knows they do. Considering everything she's been through in these past two days, they had every right to be worried about her doing this.

She's tempted to text or call them, just to tell them that she's alright, but then she sees the most recent text. Her eyes widen. "Guys," she says, "I think our parents are already there."

Rev plays a wrong note.

Cass has to stop herself from slamming on the

breaks in reaction. "What the hell is that supposed to mean?" she asks in a measured tone.

"The last text from my dad. It says, 'We here with Cass and Rev's parents and Junie's aunt. Where are you?'"

"Oh, crap," Cass and Rev say at the same time.

"What are we gonna do?" Rev asks. "They're never gonna let us get on stage after we ran away. And they've probably told Junie's aunt all about it. They might never let us *see* one another after this!"

"We're screwed!" Cass says.

"We don't know any of that for sure," Shawna says. "Maybe they just came to hear us play?"

Rev and Cass both throw her flat looks.

"Yeah, we're screwed," Shawna says.

Chapter Fourteen

CASS CIRCLES AROUND THE BLOCK A COUPLE OF TIMES as soon as they get close to the club. They made it to Indianapolis with a half hour to spare, but now they have to face their parents.

"I'm never gonna be allowed to leave my room again," Rev says.

"They're gonna give me that *look* again," Cass says.

"Stop it, both of you," Shawna says. She's trying to think and Rev and Cass's constant talking is making it difficult. She can't come up with any kind of plan. She can't think of any scenario in which they can sneak past their parents to play the gig first. It's inevitable. "I think we're just gonna have to do it," she says. "Face the music."

Rev forces a chuckle. "Band humor," she says distantly.

Cass turns out of the loop she was driving in and pulls up to the club. The glowing blue neon sign declares it to be the Angry Whirlpool. In front of it is a line of three very familiar cars and five very familiar people. Rev's mom is pacing, cell phone in hand, probably trying to call Rev. Shawna's dads are holding one another, clearly distressed, along with Cass's parents.

Cass parks the van across the street. Shawna's Papa is the first to see it and points it out to the other parents. They crowd around, concern so palpable that the bandmates can feel it through the walls of the van. They take a deep breath together and Shawna steps out first.

She is immediately enveloped in a tight hug from both of her parents.

"Oh my God, oh my God, we were so worried

about you, oh my God," her Papa repeats over and over again. He sounds like he's trying not to cry.

"Why did you do this? You could have ended up dead in a ditch somewhere!" her Dad says. She doesn't think he expects a real answer.

"I'm sorry," Shawna says, hugging them back. She's beginning to cry, as well.

Rev steps out of the van next.

"Margaret! Oh, my god!" her mom says, "What the hell is *wrong* with you, child!" She pulls her already crying daughter into a hug and begins an emotion-fueled lecture.

— — —

On the driver's side, Cass's mother has broken down in tears upon seeing that her child is alive and Cass's father is asking Cass every question he can think to ask about her well-being. Cass is already rolling her eyes. She gets concerned looks from her mother and concerned questions from her father every time she leaves her parents' sight.

"Alright, alright, I'm fine!" Cass says, breaking into the tirade. "I survived a little road trip! *Wow! Shocking!*" She is stopped from making any more sarcastic comments by a lump in her throat. Her parents aren't the best. Heck, at some level, they really suck as parents. They are overbearing and overprotective, believing Cass can't do anything because of her disability, but Cass just wants a hug right now. A long, long hug. Then she can go back to being mad at them.

Her mother pulls her into a hug before she can give into the urge herself, and she doesn't resist. She lets her parents help her into her chair and continues to hug them both, doing her best to tune out whatever stupid thing is being said.

– – –

When everyone is all cried and hugged out, the real lecturing starts. The bandmates are told how stupid the whole trip was, how disrespectful it was to run away, how they're all underage and how they know nothing of the world yet.

In the midst of this, a woman walks up to the group. She leans against the van and listens for a moment. "You see, this is why it's important to get parental permission," she says. The whole group turns to her. She wiggles her fingers at them with a smile.

The woman has short-cropped blue hair and light-brown skin. The shade of her lips and nails matches her hair perfectly. The silver bangles she wears around her wrists tinkle as she moves and her earrings hang down so low they almost brush her shoulders. Junie's aunt Nelle. The Angry Whirlpool belongs to her.

"I have to say, kiddos, I'm a little disappointed in you," she says, taking a few steps forward, her smile hardly wavering. "You said that parental permission was no problem. Then again, I suppose it wouldn't be if you never got it." She chuckles. Altogether, she seems far too nonchalant for the situation. "Now, lying and manipulation are wrong. I'm sure you all know that," she says.

The bandmates nod, all their focus on her. Sure, their parents can yell and ground them and make them feel guilty for what they've done, but they can't actually stop them from getting onto that stage. The Beauty School Dropouts have come this far. They're not going to be deterred by parental disapproval. Only Nelle has the final word.

"However," Nelle says, "seeing as all of your parents are here with us, right now, we may be able to come to some sort of understanding." She looks to their parents. Their parents look at her and then back at their children.

Shawna steps forward first. "Dad, Papa," she says, "I know we messed up. We shouldn't have disobeyed you, and I'm sorry. But we've come all this way. It's just . . . it feels like it would be a waste to just quit now."

Her parents look at one another. She can see in her

Papa's eyes that he's struggling, not wanting to crush his little girl's dreams. Her Dad seems to be, as well.

Cass, having gotten past all the mushy stuff, is glaring at her parents, daring them to tell her no.

"Well, you all do whatever you want with your own children. Margaret is coming home with me," Rev's mom says.

"Mom, *please* . . . " Rev says.

"No!" her mom says. "This is ridiculous. You didn't even tell me that you had been offered something like this."

Shawna and Cass look over to Rev. She had told them that her mom had said "no," not that she had never even asked her.

"I knew you would have said 'no,'" Rev mutters.

"And *you!*" Rev's mom looks over to Nelle, not even acknowledging what Rev said. "Why the hell didn't you think to contact us? They're minors! Honestly!"

Nelle smiles and shrugs. "Guess I just trust too easily," she says. "Besides, I didn't have your numbers."

Rev's mom huffs. She grabs her daughter's arm and starts to pull her away. "Come on. We're going home."

Rev pulls her arm out of her mother's grasp. "No," she says, planting her feet and straightening her posture.

"*What* did you just say to me?" her mom says.

"I-I said *no!*" Rev says. "This is really, really important to me, Mom. I-I love this band, and I want to . . . I want to do this. I *want to do this.*"

"Oh, don't be stupid," her mom says, rolling her eyes. "You won't care about this at all in a couple of years, and then you'll be glad that I dragged you home and set you straight. And remember your stage fright? I'm just looking out for you."

Rev cringes for a moment, but then Shawna takes her hand. She squeezes it and gives Rev a little smile. Cass is giving Rev's mom the same glare she gives people who pity her. They're both behind her, both in her corner.

"No, you're not," Rev says. "You're always telling me that I'm too stupid or weak to do things. You've never supported me, not once, and I'm not gonna let you bully me into thinking that I can't do this, because I can! I know I can."

Her mother is staring at Rev, mouth open. "How dare you talk to me like that, young lady? I am your *mother*," she says. "You get in the car, *right now*."

"No," Rev says. She squeezes Shawna's hand tighter. Shawna has never seen her speak to her mother like this.

"Alright, *fine*," her mom says. "Be like that. Be selfish. I have been worried sick about you for the past two days, but *fine*! Go and play with your little band and leave me alone to contemplate what a *terrible* mother I am. Go on! You can find your own ride back home." She storms back to her car and gets in, slamming the door behind her. She starts the car and drives away.

Rev is clearly trying not to cry.

Shawna pulls her into a hug. "It's okay," she says. "That was great. You did great. You're not being stupid or selfish or anything."

"Yeah, Rev!" Cass says. "That was totally awesome! For real!"

"I told you there was something I didn't like about that woman," Shawna's Dad mutters to her Papa, just loud enough for everyone to hear.

"Well, I choose to take that as permission," Nelle says. "What about the rest of you? I'll throw in free admission for you to watch your kids play."

Their parents are silent, each thinking while Rev does her best to calm down.

Shawna's Dad is the first to speak up. "Okay, look," he says, "I can see that you all understand that what you did was wrong. You disobeyed us and you could have gotten yourselves hurt. However, I have to admit that it's hard not to be proud that you managed to pull it off."

Smiles creep onto each of the bandmates' faces.

Shawna's dad turns to the other parents. "Clearly this means a lot to them," he says. "Maybe we refused to understand just how much, or maybe they're all just spoiled, rebellious teenagers . . . "

Shawna giggles. Her dad is making jokes. That's always a good sign.

" . . . but I just can't tell them 'no.' And maybe that's part of the problem, but I've never seen a Beauty School Dropouts performance, and I feel like I'm missing out. We can always ground them later."

Shawna's Papa is smiling at him. Cass's parents seem to be going over it in their minds, the cogs visibly turning.

"I . . . I don't know . . . " Cass's mom says.

"Please, mom," Cass says. The woman's eyes widen in surprise. So do Shawna's. Cass being polite to her parents is also something she's never seen.

Cass's mom turns to her husband. "What do you think, honey?" she asks.

"I . . . " he says, then sighs. "Alright. Yeah. Go do your thing." He smiles at Cass and Cass, for once, smiles back at him.

"Excellent!" Nelle says, smiling and clapping her hands together. She glances at her watch. "I'll have to push your stage time back a few minutes so you have time to set up, but that won't be a problem."

She puts two fingers in her mouth and whistles. Two buff women march out of the club and start unloading the back of the van. Nelle hops into the arms of a third. "Follow me, kiddos!" She laughs like a nineties anime villain as she is carried to the club's back entrance.

The bandmates and their parents stare after her for a few moments, but the bandmates decide that they have seen weirder in the past forty-eight hours.

"Livin' the dream," Shawna says with a shrug. She leads her friends to the back entrance, excitement bubbling in her chest.

Chapter Fifteen

THE GUITAR SINGS, AND SHAWNA SINGS ALONG WITH it. She feels her heart beating to the rhythm Cass is banging out. There are lights, there are people, there's a microphone in her hand that didn't come from a thrift store. She's on a stage, a real stage, singing Rev's lyrics about running away. Her parents are in the audience, cheering for her. Cass's are there, too. Rev's mom is mercifully absent. The crowd cheers for them, loving every minute, loving the Beauty School Dropouts. They even call for an encore.

Well, five days ago, they did. Today, Shawna sits alone in her room, bored out of her skull. Her dads grounded her for three weeks. Cass's parents grounded her for four and Rev's mom . . . well, the situation is complicated, at best. She spends a lot of time at Shawna's house, now. After her mother's little outburst, Shawna's dads encourage it.

Shawna hears her phone *ping*. An email. She picks it up to see an address she doesn't recognize and the subject It's Cici.

She fumbles with her phone and opens it immediately.

Hey, Shawna!

I found a part of your show on YouTube. (Attached is a link to the video). You guys are awesome! I'm so glad you were able to make it to your gig. It looked like the crowd loved you.

The cops finally raided my place because of those crackheads, and I had to bounce. It's whatever, really. I mean, I'm pretty pissed, but I can find another place. I'll be okay.

You probably shouldn't come looking for me. It's pretty dangerous and stuff. I don't want you getting hurt or in trouble, but who knows? Maybe fate has other plans. But probably not.

Goodbye.

-Cici

Shawna stares at the email, reading it and rereading it at least four times. She closes it and starts to do as much research as she can on her phone about underage homelessness.

Over the next week, she compiles a list of helpful links and numbers and locations. She sends it to Cici's email address. She tells Cici that she shouldn't give up, that Shawna is in her corner. She describes everything that happened on the crazy road trip and encourages her to keep in touch. She concludes it with her address and full name.

She anxiously waits around the house for another week, checking her phone every couple of minutes.

Once she is released from her grounding, her phone checking dies down a little. The email continues to hang around in the back of her mind, though, and for the rest of the summer she wonders if Cici ever got it. She wonders what she's doing, where she's staying, if she's okay.

She doesn't get her answers until three days before school begins. She and Cass are helping Rev check things off of a list, helping her calm down and making sure she has everything, when there's a ping on her phone. She opens her phone and the ping turns out to be from an email she doesn't recognize with a .edu address. The subject says It's Cici. She gasps.

"What?" Cass asks.

"Cici!" Shawna says. "The girl from the motel!"

"She finally emailed you back?" Rev asks.

"'Bout time," Cass groans. "You've been yapping about that girl all summer. What's so important about her, anyway?"

Shawna doesn't answer, just opens the email.

Hey,

School address. They just give these out to us. It's nice.

Thanks for that comprehensive list you sent me a while back. Been reading through. Didn't have much time to research before. It was a good start. Sorry I never emailed you back till now. It would've made your offer to crash at your place too tempting. I can't do that to you.

I'm gonna be going to school again, though. Don't know how that will help, but it's what everyone says to do. At least I'm staying in a place that's not going to send me back home. And there's food here!

Don't worry about me too much, okay?

-Cici

Shawna doesn't read this one through as many times, but she does give it a second look. She imagines herself on the run for real. She imagines herself getting ready for the school year without Rev or Cass or the budget for most of the things on the list Cass is holding. She imagines not coming home, not hugging her dads, not knowing if the place she's staying is going to kick her out or send her into a dangerous situation. She imagines just being provided with food being worthy of an exclamation point.

She looks up at her friends. None of their crazy road trip would have been possible without the safety net their families provided. Maybe they need to stop singing about running away with such wistfulness.

She looks back to her phone and types out a quick reply. She sends her support again and tells Cici she's proud of her. She tells her to come visit, if she can, and tells her that she'll come visit her if Cici wants. She asks Cici to tell her if she needs anything, and that any kind of keeping in touch is wonderful, no matter how long the time gap. After she sends it, she looks back up to her friends.

"If there's ever a benefit concert for youth homelessness, I want to be a part of it," Shawna says.

She must have said it with some level of severity, because Rev and Cass don't say anything back. They just nod.

After a few moments of silence, though, Cass lets out a small chuckle. "Heh. 'Stay in School!' featuring the Beauty School Dropouts!" she says.

Rev snorts and starts to giggle.

Shawna just smiles at them both and plucks the school list out of Cass's hands. She looks it over, intending to buy doubles of everything and find a shelter to send them to.